A CASTLE
OF BONE

Also by Penelope Farmer
CHARLOTTE SOMETIMES

A CASTLE OF BONE

PENELOPE FARMER

RED FOX

A Red Fox Book

Published by Random House Children's Books
20 Vauxhall Bridge Road, London SW1V 2SA

A division of Random House UK Ltd
London Melbourne Sydney Auckland
Johannesburg and agencies throughout the world

Copyright © Penelope Farmer 1972, 1992

1 3 5 7 9 10 8 6 4 2

First published in Great Britain by
Chatto and Windus Ltd 1972

This edition with revisions, first published in 1992 by
The Bodley Head Children's Books
Red Fox edition 1999

Printed and bound in Norway by
AiT Trondheim AS

Papers used by Random House UK Limited are natural, recyclable products
made from wood grownin sustainable forests. The manufacturing processes
conform to the environmental regulations of the country of origin.

RANDOM HOUSE UK Limited Reg. No. 954009

ISBN 0 09 926718 7

For Judy with love,
and for Sandy Hayhurst
who made writing this book possible.

. . .And bones of solidness froze
Over all his nerves of joy . . .

            — WILLIAM BLAKE

The achievement of Manwyddan the wise
After lamentation and fiery wrath
Was a construction of the bone fortress of
   Oeth and Anoeth.   — WELSH TRIAD

CHAPTER ONE

"What's that noise?" asked Jean. They all stood staring at the cupboard. Penn against the light looked huge – his hair edged by light, blazed, caught sun, almost reflected it.

"What noise?" Penn asked.

"But there's nothing," Hugh said, "except my wallet." Penn's sister Anna had just put it there, then closed the cupboard door.

"Oh wait, oh *listen*," timid Anna said.

And there was a noise; very small at first; rustlings, tappings, scrapings – but gradually louder, like a tree Hugh thought, a tree growing inside the cupboard, its branches dragging, rapping against the door, blown by some hidden wind. In a moment the sound, increasing, was of neither tree nor wind, it was a huge sound booming within those narrow wooden walls, some huge form banging and racketing in there. And he heard another sound also, as loud as the first, but tighter, shriller, which sounded, only it could not be, like the squealing of a pig.

Penn as usual took Hugh's decision for him; leaned forward, pulled open both the cupboard doors; within the instant of the click a large white sow fell out, rolled over, picked itself up and blundered, terrified, across the room – quite unmistakably a real pig, with hanging dugs and crude, pre-historic-looking skin; Hugh, though dazed, could see the little bristles that edged its ears, saw the blue symbol stamped on its flank, like the price

mark stamped on supermarket goods; as it missed
Anna by inches, knocked over his cluttered
chair –

"Hugh, the *door*, watch out," Penn yelled, too
late, because the pig which had not for one
moment ceased to squeal, dashed through, turned
sideways and fell down the first and narrowest
flight of stairs. Hugh diving to Penn's shout, was
unable to check the movement of his hand, slammed the door shut, and as he opened it again the
pig fell down more stairs, crashed with full bulk,
dangerously, against quivering bannisters, careered
along the landing, down a third flight, thundered
its feet on the wooden hall floor then shot out of
the door into the front garden, Penn and the others
in confused pursuit.

Hugh saw Jean's cat bolt upright on a flowerbed
watching them; he saw the pig now lurching but
still swift enough, run out through the open garden
gate. Jean was wailing like a little girl.

"It'll get run over, it'll get run over."

"We'd better try heading it to the park,"
shrieked Penn.

The gate crashed shut behind them with a clash
of iron. The wooden fence shivered all along its
length. The black cat watching had not shifted
fractionally.

"Your ma must have heard," Penn was saying
breathlessly to Hugh.

"She might not. I think she's out. Jesus, just
look at it" – he saw the pig weave erratically across
the road – "something's going to hit it *soon*."

"At least they slow down here – but on the main

road . . ." Penn took speed again. Ahead of him the pig took speed too, its tail uncurled by speed streaming out behind, and by good luck turned right (the way they needed if they were to drive it towards the park), first kept to the pavement for twenty yards or so, then swerved diagonally towards the traffic island in the middle of the road, where at last it paused. Perhaps the blink of the orange beacons had bewildered it. A car almost halted at the crossing too; thought better of it, jerked on; the pig as immediately decided to move. Pig squeal met brake squeal – whether pig actually met car was impossible to tell, but its flight continued more furiously than ever, while everywhere along the road people stopped and turned and heads shot from cars. Anna and Jean slowed, panting. Hugh entangled himself with a woman and a yellow dog. Even Penn was not close enough to head the pig up the first road leading to the park, and would have failed at the second probably, had not the pig itself swerved wildly and taken that road of its own accord.

There was a gate at the far end. It was designed to keep deer from getting out of the park, so might not normally have let in a pig, only a man happened to be holding it open for a woman with a pram. Neither noticed the pig until it careered past them; at which the startled man let the gate swing back, barring the pig's exit to the road, but leaving its entrance clear into the park. It ran itself once, frantically, into the iron bars. The second time freely, easily, it ran out, through the trees towards a patch of summer bracken – white pig they saw, black trees, green bracken. Then the pig vanished. They did not see it any more. Almost at once they ceased to hear it squeal.

CHAPTER TWO

It had taken Hugh and his father most of the morning to find that cupboard. Hugh's room had sloping corners and a window looking into the ash tree, but till now it had had no cupboard, and in one of her periodic domestic agitations his mother had declared that he needed one and sent them both out to look. Hugh, having better things to do with a Saturday at the beginning of the summer holidays, argued that he had hung his clothes on hooks for years, so what, suddenly, was wrong with hooks now? And if he must have a cupboard, why did he, Hugh, have to help look for it? A cupboard was a cupboard, was a cupboard. He did not mind what it looked like. His father said that hooks were adequate but cupboards better; that Hugh with his artistic pretensions should know better than anyone that function should not be divorced from appearance, and if he did not know this was it not about time he learnt? Furthermore, he said, jamming on the battered green felt hat that he wore regardless, both winter and summer, he was not basically interested in buying a cupboard for Hugh either; a fact Hugh would never have guessed from the amount of unlikely and unsuitable shops he seemed prepared to explore in search of it.

They had found themselves at last, both hot and cross and bored, outside a junk shop in a little street that ran down towards the river. There was a trestle table on the pavement with a heap of old music sheets on it, torn and dog-eared, another heap of scratched 78–speed records, a tray of battered, shineless jewellery, chipped plates, chipped cups, stacked precariously, also a cardboard box which said 6X20 Country Vegetable in two-inch-high blue letters and held an assortment of bleached and dusty books. ANTIQUES the board above the door said. "Junk," shouted Hugh's father, striding under the board and into the shop, turning impatiently to beckon Hugh after him.

Inside Hugh sneezed twice, rapidly. It was at least as radical a change of environment as would have been plunging under the sea. Every sense shocked, retreated, reorganized itself. His skin at chill produced goose pimples, his nose sneezed at dust and mould and damp and another, sweeter, but as aged smell, and his eyes seemed to fade in the dim, furred, almost tangible light. To his ears the sounds that escaped from the outside world seemed distorted, like sounds at the far end of a narrow tunnel.

Never in his life had he seen so many things crammed into so small a space – furniture piled up, pictures fitted together on the walls without an inch between them, every table and chair heaped with smaller objects, spoons and ornaments and candlesticks, fans and necklaces, inkwells and ash trays, books and more records. Even the ceiling was crowded, hung with chairs and tables, like angular creepers, among which Hugh's father had to duck his head. The shop altogether was like a forest, Hugh thought, a close dark jungle. But a forest without life; nothing moved in it. For a moment with a shock Hugh saw a white face

watching them, but it was a china face on a china
head, with blind white eyes and a pale, straw-like
wig.

There was a gramophone as well as records.
Hugh would not have recognized the rectangular
black box, but his father did. Snatching a record
from the pile and setting it on the green baize
turntable, he fitted a handle into a slot and wound
up the gramophone. As the turntable spun round,
scratchy but lively music began to jitter across the
shop.

The old man stood between a low cupboard and
a tall chair watching them. They did not see him
come, nor where he had come from. There were
gaps between objects, here and there, but nothing
as defined as a doorway, though there must have
been some way into the back of the shop, Hugh
thought.

"We're looking for a cupboard," he shouted,
guiltily, above the music. For his father, jigging to
it, rapturously, still seemed to have noticed
nothing. "That cupboard," he said pointing. His
eyes fleeing beyond the old man, he had noticed
the cupboard for the first time.

The old man had come nearer then and taken
off the needle arm and stopped the gramophone.
The music left a shadow of itself, then was altogether gone. Yet it was still, to that, to the sound
of something called Dinah's Ragtime Boogie – con-
juring from some unexpected corner of his
memory irrelevant images of feathered and beaded
ladies jigging rhythmically among potted palms –
that Hugh saw it – his cupboard – for the first
time.

Immediately he had never in his life wanted anything as much as he wanted that, not even his first box of proper oil paints.

It was extraordinary that he could have wanted the cupboard so much. "It's monstrous, abominable," his father said. And Hugh could not have denied it if he tried. Yet that had not made any difference to him. And his father was so bored with the search by now that he did not bother to argue the point for long; at least it was a cupboard and cheap at that. A cupboard he had, after all, been instructed to find.

CHAPTER THREE

The houses were joined, a pair, tall, pointed and curious; either unsymmetric without the other. Their windows had stonework like eyebrows over them. Along this road all the houses were in pairs but no pair was like any other one, the gables different in particular, some as curvilinear and plump as in this pair they were angular and sharp. The right-hand house had recently been converted and Penn and Anna's parents had bought the flat made of the top two floors. All the paint on this house was new, builders' sand and ladders still littering the garden at the front of it. But Hugh's and Jean's parents had lived in the whole of the left-hand house as long as Jean at least could remember, and it had not been painted for easily as long as that. The paint was a faded pink, the stonework yellowish. Rhubarb and custard Penn called it when he wanted to annoy Hugh.

The cupboard arrived there that evening, long after Hugh had given up hope of it. The sun – a fire between crimson and scarlet – squatted on the skyline as they carried it in through the garden gate; two men in stained white aprons, oily-headed, who mopped themselves and complained bitterly, in dualogue, when it came to lugging the thing up three flights of Victorian stairs. How in all the supernatural .- . . could it be so heavy they wondered, and indeed Hugh wondered too, for as cupboards go it did not look particularly heavy. Its doors, swung open, looked thin as matchboard.

"Shoddy, there you are, Hugh, I told you so," declared his father with gloomy satisfaction. "Ain't known another like it, for weight not," the balder of the two men said as he closed his fingers round Hugh's father's inevitably flamboyant tip.

"It's hideous, monstrous," Hugh's father said with enjoyment, examining the cupboard carefully again.

But when Hugh went to bed that night, his clothes were still strewn about the room. He did not know what had stopped him putting them away in the cupboard. Not laziness certainly, though he was usually lazy about such things. But some odd reluctance that he did not try to explain.

And in bed, when he shut his eyes, the empty cupboard assumed . . . in the darkness . . . What it assumed did not frighten, so much as exhilarate him; his heart thumped extraordinarily. Yet he would not let himself analyse what he felt, he forced his mind away into pictures, images.

He began to try to visualize the cupboard. He had tried before, that morning, after they had bought it. His father had decided to have a drink and Hugh had sat on the wall overlooking the river with a glass of Coca-cola beside him, trying to remember what the cupboard looked like.

But he had not been able to. If momentarily he had caught some detail, immediately he had attempted to fit another to it, it would slide away again. He had had a very strong feeling of it, yet could not translate this visually; which had annoyed him because as a rule he was not only observant, but practised consciously retaining what he observed, in order to use it in his painting. He had come to do this almost automatically. Yet now in bed though he had seen the cupboard once again, when he tried to visualize it, still no picture came into his mind.

Instead he saw other images from that morning beside the river: the Coca-cola – a dark elliptical liquid in the glass with a small white moon in it of reflected light – when he had raised his eyes from that, there had been across the river a group of trees, and now in bed that image crowded out the nearer one. They were a group of willows and alders, the alders darker, dourer-looking than the pollarded willow trees.

The group seemed to be closing in on him, rushing towards him through his head. In a moment he could focus on one tree only, in a moment more could see only an area of trunk quite close to him. He reached out a hand, involuntarily. He touched wood. His fingers scraped on, scraped up, wood bark. He opened his eyes. He was standing among alder trees, facing one trunk, one tree. When he took his hand away from it there was green, from the bark, beneath his fingernails.

The trees that morning which had stood in line, now encircled him, and there were no willows, only alder trees – there was a fire too in the middle of the grove, burning fiercely, with hints of blue and green flame. A girl sat by the fire, feeding it big and little sticks. Hugh could not see her face because her head was bent away from him, but she had very black, very straight, hair and a red dress and bare white feet.

He realized that he himself was still wearing pyjamas. Seeing the girl, he clutched the jacket

about him for it was flapping open, having lost all
but one of its buttons. (He had told his mother
about the buttons, several times – "Oh, I'll sew
them on for you, love," she had said each time,
but the jacket had always come back from being
washed, neatly folded but still buttonless. Jean
would have sewed them on, if he had asked, but
Hugh had never remembered to ask her.)

The girl made no move. She did not look at
Hugh. He was not even sure that she had noticed
him. The river ran beyond the alder grove, and on
the other side of it, near the bridge, a man stood
fishing. Beyond the river was the hill.

There was no town now. The hill was bare
except for a few trees, and on top of it a square
and turreted castle. The falling sun caught one side
fleetingly and made the turrets look as if they had
been painted red.

The instant Hugh saw this castle he knew he had
to reach it. He began to move but meanwhile the
girl poked at the fire so violently that it glared for
a moment with brilliant light, with particularly
bright and fiery heat, and the heat felt like a wall
through which he had to break. It receded behind
him afterwards. Immediately he pulled himself
through what felt like another wall – of what he
did not know, only that it was hostile to him –
and so passed out of the ring of alder trees.

He did not look at the girl again. He had never
properly seen her face, but the way she had moved
stirred some memory in him, which was quickly
gone.

He crossed the river then, by the bridge, not the
arched stone bridge that he knew, but a flat

wooden one, standing on wooden piles driven into the river-bed. Though broad enough to take a cart or chariot it had no sides to it. It felt curiously comfortable and warm to Hugh's bare feet, as if it was alive, with warm blood in it.

The sun was vanishing behind the hill. Clutching his jacket round him Hugh went on, through chillier air and fading light, thorns and stones attacking his feet, his legs beginning to ache. He could not see the castle any more. It might have been the slope which hid his view, it might have been the growing darkness. He went on anyway, climbing steeply now.

CHAPTER FOUR

The next morning, Sunday, Hugh's mother at breakfast pointed out what dirty nails he had.

"They're green, Hugh. They're disgusting. Whatever have you been doing?"

Hugh thought: I had green nails in my dream.

His mother did not often notice such things. But when she did it was with a vehemence that made him immediately rebellious, even about things to which he was usually indifferent. He and his mother were like two loose ends of charged wire these days, touched together they sparked dramatically. So now, he rushed from the kitchen, shouting, and ran upstairs as noisily as he could, slamming the bathroom door on his way past.

The noise chastened him a little. He flung himself down on his bed with a feeling of anti-climax, regretting his half-eaten and now unobtainable breakfast. Almost immediately he picked himself up and went down to the bathroom on the half-landing and scrubbed his nails clean. By the time he started back upstairs to his room, he was feeling perfectly calm, though the tips of his fingers were smarting.

At the third step up he began to have a most odd sensation. He had been thinking about the cupboard, waiting empty, in his room. And suddenly it was as if the idea of it had gone outside his mind; it was as if it was pulling him from his room, while at the same time something else tried to drag him back. This something Hugh recognized after a moment as his own alarm; making him resist the pull ahead, as the gravity of an object makes it resist the contrary pull of a magnet, until he recognized what it was; then, fear lessening, the pull became irresistible and he went on up and in. To find what? Nothing as far as he could tell that was not entirely ordinary. The sun had sought out and lit the cupboard making it look cheaper, more featureless than ever. A bird shifted in the ash tree outside the window. In order to create some movement, anything, to release and justify the tension he had felt, Hugh picked up a shirt and flung it on his unmade bed.

Shortly afterwards Penn arrived to see Hugh and with him Anna, to see Jean. All of them drifted into Hugh's room to look at the new cupboard.

"It's not much to look at, is it though?" Jean had said.

The pig emerged from the cupboard not long afterwards.

When the pig had finally disappeared, they continued walking through the park. No one suggested it – no one at first said anything. They had just looked at each other and walked on, over rough grass and reddish, stony paths. Even Penn had lost his ebullience, and Jean did not attempt her usual underrunning commentary of sensible suggestions and sensible explanations. They were all stunned; partly by fear, not so much of the pig itself, but of its inexplicable appearance; partly by simple astonishment. They were much more frightened now than previously because at first there had been no time for fear.

"What would we have done with it if we had caught it?" Penn said, at last. "Perhaps it's just as well we didn't."

"We couldn't possibly have caught it," Jean said.

They were walking on open ground just here, at almost the highest point of the park. Two men were trying to fly kites – South American bird kites – scarlet, widespread, magnificent. But there was scarcely enough wind, the birds tugged up occasionally as if about to soar, then more often dipped, fluttered, dived back to earth.

"As if they were wounded," Anna said. They went through a gate into the plantation. There was a stream there and water plants, rushes and irises and orange flags, and trees, birch trees mostly, dappled, insubstantial-looking, some black and white, others with bark as satiny and wood as rough, but with a russet, even purplish sheen on them; trees like snake skin, Hugh thought.

"Like giraffe's legs," Anna said.

"Whatever are you talking about?" Penn asked.

"Enormously tall giraffes," said Hugh.

"They mean the birch trees, I think," said Jean.

"Don't be an idiot, Ann," Penn spoke with such scorn that Hugh came in to rescue Anna, though it was impossible to tell from her face whether she needed rescuing or not.

"What do you think happened, Penn? That pig, I mean."

"I can't believe it did happen. It's impossible," said Penn.

"But it did; we know it did," said Jean.

"Of course I know it happened. I never said it didn't. I just said it seems impossible. There must be some logical explanation. There always is a logical reason if you look hard enough. You'd think a car impossible if you didn't look inside the bonnet."

"Clever Penn," said Jean, a mixture of admiration and sarcasm in her voice. Perhaps, just, admiration more.

"It could have been magic," Anna said.

"Oh, *Ann*. I *said*. There must be some logical explanation."

"Well, how else did a pig appear in an empty cupboard?" asked Jean.

"We all saw it was empty," added Hugh.

"It could have come upstairs . . ." But even Penn knew that it had not. "It could have come in at the door," he suggested defiantly. "Who was looking at the door? No one was."

"Oh, come off it," said Hugh. "A thing that size. And you heard what a racket it made afterwards."

"Magic," said Anna, looking obstinate. Hugh had never known her speak as much as she had today. Normally she never said anything, not when he was around anyway, and she looked timid, even terrified; she appeared the opposite of Penn, negative to his positive, a small shadow beside his large sun.

"Well I don't believe in magic," Jean said.

"Not like some," interrupted Penn.

"But I just don't see how else . . ."

"Suppose it was just a hallucination after all."

"Suppose we imagined it. Suppose it never really happened."

Hugh, looking round him now, could almost

have believed Penn, almost wanted to believe him. They had reached a space of emerald grass fringed by more silver birches and rowan trees. The grass was too green, too soft, too smooth; the rowan berries scarlet, the tree trunks speckled black and white. It looked as unreal as elfland, Hugh thought, a place to which men were enticed in fairy tales and from which they never returned – like Sir Orfeo, or Thomas the Rhymer – except that both those had returned at last.

There were other people here and a dog or two, walking across the grass; but they dissolved into the landscape, they seemed no more real than it. Not even time seemed real any more to Hugh. Thomas and Sir Orfeo had left time as well as space when they went to fairyland, and now he and Penn and Jean and Anna were outside time too because what had happened could not belong to time, which was reality, or the reality they understood. The pig must be a hallucination. It had to be.

But even as he thought that, Hugh remembered it; its bulk, its thunderous careering, the smell and sound of it, the bristles on its skin. This place might seem unreal, but nothing could have looked more real than the pig, or been more real.

"Oh come off it, Penn. It was real all right. Anyway four people don't have the same hallucination all at once."

"Okay. Let's say it was real then." Penn bent down, picked up a birch twig, folded back his body and with it his right arm, and hurled with perfect ease and rhythm. They saw the twig arc, collide with other trees, pass among their branches with uneven percussive sounds, then fall, losing momentum, to meet ground at last. The flickering leaves of birch, like Penn's flickering red gold hair, gave an illusion of light, though the sun had disappeared.

Anna, Hugh noticed, intently watched Penn throw. When he had finished Penn glanced at her, but by then, hastily, she had looked away.

Anna's face took on an odd misshapen look as they were walking towards home again. Penn, noticing, told her sharply to stop chewing her tongue. It made her look even more hideous than usual, he said.

Jean said, "Oh that's what she's doing, is it? I've often wondered."

"She's always doing it. It makes Mum wild, you can see why."

"It helps me think, that's all," Anna said. She dropped behind them and walked along the path alone. Hugh could not forget her at his back, she felt a weight on his heels, a load, almost oppressing him. He thought that was because he felt sorry for her, Penn having been so fierce, and at last he too held back to let her catch him up. Penn and Jean went on a little ahead of them, Penn flicking neatly at grasses with a stick.

"What were you thinking, Anna?" Hugh asked.

Anna did not reply.

"Anything might help. Anything you thought of – however unlikely. Everything seems unlikely now."

"Your wallet, the one I put in the cupboard. What was it made of?"

"Why did you put it in the cupboard, Anna? – a wallet? Of all things . . ."

"I don't know. Why shouldn't I put something in. It was empty, the cupboard," Anna said. When Hugh looked at her he could not see her face at all. Her head was bent. Her dark hair swung down.

His wallet was so old and familiar he had scarcely looked at it for years. To remember it properly he had to think quite hard. Inside and out it had been a pale, pinkish colour, darkened in some places more than others by both age and dirt. Its edges had been whipped with a narrow thong.

"Leather," he said.

"And leather is . . ."

"Skin, of course," Penn turned, overhearing them.

"Anna wondered what my wallet was."

"What sort of skin?" Anna asked.

"Horse skin, cow skin, sheep skin," Penn said.

"Deer skin," Hugh said. They had left the park by now and were passing a pub called The Roebuck. A roedeer leapt across the faded sign.

"What about your wallet anyway?" asked Jean.

"Well, Anna put in the cupboard and the next thing was the pig came out."

"That doesn't mean your wallet had anything to do with it."

"What sort of leather was it?" insisted Anna, obstinately.

"I don't know," Hugh said. "It's so old. It was Dad's first, then mine."

"We'll have a look when we get back," said Penn. "But I don't suppose it's relevant."

But the cupboard was empty. They thought the

pig in its rush must have knocked the wallet out.
They hunted everywhere for it, peering under
chairs, under the bed, crawling on hands and
knees. But they could not find it.

"It would be easier, Hugh, if your room was
tidier," Jean said. "Now you've got the cupboard
why don't you put your clothes away?"

"I don't suppose it's relevant, anyway," said
Penn.

They went their separate ways. Hugh had a contented, solitary afternoon. Until the evening he
almost forgot about the cupboard. Certainly,
though he was painting, his easel set up next to it,
he did not feel the presence of it at all.

In the evening he sat on the edge of his bed
wearing his slippers and his pyjamas. His knees
jutted uncomfortably – the bed was low and his
legs of late seemed to have grown inconveniently
long. He had raised his hand and put it to the lamp,
the image of which hung infinitesimally behind his
eyes, after he had extinguished it. He did not at
once take his hand from the switch.

For in the darkness, he felt again what he had
felt on the stairs that morning; the pulling forward
and dragging back, attraction, repulsion, simultaneously. But now both impulses seemed to be
inside his head and they drew him to, drew him
from – what?

Hugh remembered last night; the image of his
Coca-cola glass displaced by the alder grove.
Tonight was different though, because he realized
he had been expecting something similar to
happen, whereas last night he had been expecting

nothing. He also had the feeling that he ought to be able to control it, at least to decide whether it happened or not. But he could only control anything to the extent that he could control himself – or rather his own mind – and how could he do that, he thought, rather resentfully, when he did not even know what his area of decision was. He let his will go anyway, with scarcely a struggle; opened his mind, grabbed a picture out of air, to have it displaced at once by trees, maddening trees, that melted from light to dark, from visibility to invisibility; birch trees, naturally.

He stood at the edge of a wood, at night, with above a silver moon and stars, and on the ground a scattering of snow. The leaf mould beneath the snow had a film of frost on it. Layers cracked lightly when he moved his feet – it was a sensation rather than a sound which made him glad he wore slippers as well as his pyjamas, though both seemed inadequate, not to say ridiculous, for such a time and place. Fortunately Jean had yesterday sewn his buttons on, so he was able at least to do the jacket up.

He was quite alone this time. He looked back almost hopefully into the birch wood in case the girl was there. But he saw only moon-made lights and shadows that looked as bright and as dark, alternately, as the trunks of the trees themselves.

Ahead was a bare and empty country; oddly magnified, in sweeps and hollows, with what might have been a track but masked by snow. In the distance as he expected stood the castle, and he stepped out towards it knowing that he must. But stopped almost at once, abruptly; first startled, then, for a moment, terrified.

There was something black lying in the snow. He had noticed it but not taken in what it was since it lay motionless, well to the right of the direction he had to take. But now from the corner of an eye he saw it move, and as he swung round towards it, heard an uncanny cry that left him tight with fear. The black thing divided. Part wheeled up and rode away, calling, on the air – a crow, Hugh thought. It made other cruel and unearthly sounds. But at least he recognized what it was.

Reluctantly he altered his path a little and went towards the black thing that remained behind.

It was another crow, but dead. Black feathers lay on the white snow and drops of fresh blood. Red blood, thought Hugh, though the moonlight had bleached the colour out. He thought of the black-haired girl in the red dress with a strange nostalgic kind of ache, feeling suddenly lonelier than in all his life before.

He shook himself. He went on, alone, towards the castle. It looked almost transparent tonight, it might have been made of glass or ice. In places the walls were so white, so staring, they were like mirrors reflecting moonlight, while elsewhere they were so black it was as if Hugh looked right through them to the night sky itself. There were even little points of light upon the black, that could have been the stars.

He seemed to see patterns spiralling up the turrets nearest him; or they could have been staircases mounting within transparent walls, but no matter how much he strained his eyes he could not have said for certain which.

The moon had come to seem particular, like a lamp to guide a traveller to the castle.

On went Hugh, stumbling over rough ground, with tufts of grass which tipped and emptied snow into his bedroom slippers, having to pick his way so carefully that he took his eyes from the castle ahead of him. Meanwhile clouds crept up, unnoticed, to engulf the moon. It rode among them visibly at first, though dimmed. Then it was altogether gone. When Hugh looked up again he could not see the castle any more.

He could not see anything. Not only the castle had gone but the wood behind him. The wind had risen – winds drove around Hugh, needled and bit him, rent and buffeted. Snow seemed to whirl at him from all the corners of the world. Then he shut his eyes and there was only dark. He felt his knees humped up, his feet jammed hard against the floor. They were icy and his slippers sopping wet. He took his hand from the electric switch, toppled into bed, dragged his blankets round him and slept all night, exhausted, and with wet slippers on.

CHAPTER FIVE

Hugh and Penn were in some ways the most unlikely friends; their living next door to each other mere chance, so irrelevant to the fact that they were friends. They did not even go to the same school, and out of school their interests were entirely different. Hugh read, dreamed, gazed out of the window and drew continually, when he was not actually painting. Penn chiefly played games. He belonged to most school teams and played in scratch teams during the holidays. The rest of the time he and Hugh were inseparable, more or less.

He went to the local grammar school, Hugh to a private school, but both were in continual trouble for doing little there other than what they liked doing anyway. Thus they kept each other company at the bottom of their mediocre classes (at Hugh's school, politely, his was called Remove) though Penn did maintain even this position rather more easily, while Hugh was threatened periodically with still further demotion to a class whose master he disliked heartily, and so had to undertake furious, if short-lived, bouts of formal work.

Hugh envied mildly Penn's not needing to do the same. He was irritated occasionally by Penn's admonitions to him to buck up, pull his socks up, stir his stumps and the like. Mostly, though, he scarcely even noticed them, let the bossiness float away, evaporate.

For, much more, Hugh liked Penn's certainties. Things got started and done without his bothering to have to make up his own mind; which did not stop him exploring mentally his own rather different plans and ideas, only meant he need not risk spoiling them by putting them into action too soon or in the wrong way, so destroying patterns that he felt himself on the verge of discovering. Moreover it suited him to be left alone so much to paint while Penn was occupied with playing games.

He did not feel either superior or inferior to Penn, except in respects he did not care about. He just felt different, that was all. And he enjoyed sitting in the light of the sun that Penn represented to the world, because then people, dazzled, did not notice him. He could have done with having Penn to protect him at school, too.

What Penn saw in Hugh was much less obvious.

That morning, Monday, Penn came round after breakfast; after his breakfast, that is. (Being the holidays Hugh and Jean's mother got theirs in what she called her own time, which meant late, unless they came down and got it first.) He clattered down the stairs to the basement looking too tall for the ceiling, though he was not – Hugh was taller, and even he did not have to bend his head. Anna trailed after, looking tired and pale, in a rather short black cotton dress. She tended to wear clothes like that, which her mother chose and liked and which suited her, but which eclipsed Anna.

"Coffee, Penn?" Hugh's mother asked vaguely, from behind a newspaper, nibbling as if accidentally, at her third slice of toast.

"I don't like coffee much."

"Milk? Help yourself. Or toast."

"No thanks, I won't." Penn looked at Hugh very pointedly. "Are you nearly ready, Hugh? We've got an awful lot to talk about."

The arguments, however, had not altered since the day before, so that Jean left downstairs for a while to help wash up did not miss anything. Anna protested magic twice in a small voice, then stood by the window, gazing out, existing on the fringes of the room and of the argument. Penn was, if anything, more insistent than ever on some logical ordinary explanation for what had happened, and Hugh himself would have preferred to believe Penn today. For he had picked up one of his slippers to find it not only damp still but water-stained and with a small, dead birch leaf stuck to the crinkled rubber sole. As he could not for the life of him remember how or why this could be so, the implications both puzzled and disturbed him.

August had asserted itself after the greyness of the day before. The sun poured into Hugh's room generously, openly, and by its light the cupboard could not have appeared more commonplace and shoddy. It had been so thickly varnished that even the natural grain of the wood appeared artificial, with one door at least as golden and shiny as syrup. The other was only a little darker. "It must have had a mirror on it once," said Penn. "You can see the screw holes."

"And the glue," Hugh added; there was a trace of glue in the moulding at the top.

Inside the cupboard was no less ordinary, though less objectionable to look at, even pleasant. The wood, unvarnished, actually looked like wood, paler, pinker, and without a gloss. On the left was a row of shelves and on the right three curly brass hooks jutted above their heads. A thin brass rail ran across the top of the cupboard. There was another, thinner rail on the door for ties.

"What is it? What's it made of?" Penn asked.

"What do you think. Raffia?"

"No, platinum actually," Penn said, sarcastically.

"Gold would be prettier. Not that this is exactly pretty."

"Platinum's more valuable. I mean what *wood*, fool, idiot."

"*I* don't know," said Hugh.

"I thought you did carpentry?"

"New wood's different, it's white; well, yellowish."

"What sort of wood might you use to make a cupboard?"

"Mahogany, pine – oak . . ."

"Well which is this then?"

"It doesn't look like any of them to me. Mahogany's redder, oak's darker and much coarser-grained. I don't know otherwise. There are lots of strange African woods they use now. It could be anything."

Penn went over to the window then. Anna, very deliberately, moved away. "Could it be ash?" he asked, gazing out.

"Not possibly; it's the wrong colour. They make boats from ash, mostly anyway. It doesn't try to spring straight when you curve it, which is good for the ribs of boats."

"Gawd, aren't we knowledgeable," said Penn.

"So, what about it?" asked Hugh.

"It's a fat lot of use when you can't even tell what sort of wood this cupboard is."

Hugh went to Penn at the window. There was an acacia tree beyond the ash, its trunk split and twisted. But he had never heard of acacia furniture. Next door there was a pear tree.

"It could be fruit wood of some kind," he suggested cautiously. "You know, apple wood or pear. They have a very fine grained wood like this."

"Pretty big fruit trees. Look at the apple tree in your garden. You couldn't make a chair leg out of that, let alone a cupboard."

Anna had been moving about behind them. Suddenly they heard a click and both jumped round – Hugh momentarily surprised that he could be so easily startled, though Penn, he noticed, moved just as warily. Anna was standing by the cupboard. She was expressionless, but the cupboard doors were closed.

At that moment came another sound and Jean walked in. "What a *mess*," she said briskly. And indeed, books, clothes, papers, were strewn everywhere. Hugh thought he must have slept very untidily as well because the blankets were half off his unmade bed, and he noticed footmarks on the sheets where his slippers had been, which he covered hastily and guiltily.

"That doesn't make it look any better, Hugh," said Jean in her primmest voice.

Penn had Anna by the shoulder and was shaking her.

"What did you do, Anna? Why did you shut the cupboard?"

"I put something in. I wanted to see."

"What, Anna, what did you put in?"

"Whatever's *happening*?" begged Jean.

"It was Hugh's sweater; your red woollen one."

"My wallet was leather; pig skin," shouted Hugh, at last remembering it.

"*Pig* skin," said Anna, with triumph in her voice.

"I suppose you think," said Penn sarcastically, "I suppose you think – "

"Wool comes from sheep," Jean cried excitedly.

"Well, fancy, as if we didn't know," said Hugh.

"Well, Anna, are you expecting a sheep now?" But though Penn's voice was light, amused, he and all of them turned simultaneously to stare at the cupboard doors.

"I can't hear anything," said Jean after a moment, tentatively.

"Did you expect to? I bet nothing happens at all."

But they watched the cupboard, all of them. They waited painfully, anxiously – in hope – fear – anxiety that something would or would not come out of it. They waited for such sounds as they had heard yesterday, but there was only the commonplace chirping of the sparrows in the ash tree and the low plaint of a car coming up the road. (Hugh could tell it was up, not down, because cars going down made lighter sounds that disappeared more quickly.) The front gate clashed behind the milkman. They heard the whine and rattle of the red milk float.

Penn looked at Anna triumphantly; stared round, boldly, at the rest of them. Then he marched to the cupboard and pulled open the door. No red sweater lay on the shelf now, where Anna must have put it, only a heap of fluff such as a sheep leaves behind in a hedge; except that there was more of it and yellow; the sheep must have been recently dipped.

"You see," said Anna. "You see, Penn?"

"And you put a woollen sweater in? Are you mad, Anna, we might have got a sheep. Coping with that pig was just about enough."

"A moment ago you were saying nothing would happen. You can't have it all ways, Penn," said Hugh.

"Poor Anna," Jean said.

But Anna had begun to laugh. A moment later so had Hugh and Jean, and then, after staring round all of them in turn, slightly red-faced, rather indignant, Penn followed too, if not with much amusement. Hugh was watching Anna more; slightly pink, dishevelled, laughing, she looked quite different suddenly. She noticed his eyes and turned away, jerking her head down sideways, so that hair fell across her eyes, and when Hugh saw her face again all the colour had ebbed, leaving it as pale as usual above the short, unsuitable black dress.

They retired to the garden shortly afterwards. The sky was entirely blue, and the sun beginning to be hot. They lay full in the sun, near the old climbing frame which had half its rungs missing and leaned at an angle of forty-five degrees. Jean's cat got up from it when they appeared and took to the more adequate shade that was made by Hugh.

Penn, though still noticeably annoyed with Anna, had regained his composure and was at his bossiest; suggesting what he called a controlled experiment; they should each, he said, bring a selection of objects to put in the cupboard; they would see then what came out of it. They would have to be careful, naturally. There were things made from animals much more dangerous than pigs.

"No elephant's feet," said Jean, inclined to giggle still.

Hugh irritated by Penn took up the game at once.

"Or leopard skin."

"Or shark's teeth necklaces," said Jean.

"Sharks wouldn't be dangerous unless they brought the sea as well," said Hugh.

"Do you remember the one in the Natural History Museum? That's huge. One that size would split up the cupboard walls."

"It would split my room."

"Suppose it wouldn't get into the cupboard in the first place?" said Jean.

"How would we ever manage to explain a shark?"

Anna said nothing. Penn stiffly, red with annoyance, said they weren't here to talk about sharks, and what time would they meet that afternoon to try the cupboard out?

"No," said Hugh violently. "Not this afternoon."

"But whyever not."

"It's my room, my cupboard, isn't it? No, no, no."

Penn was silent for a moment. Both Jean and Anna appeared asleep, while Hugh stroked the cat frenetically. After a moment it twisted from his hands and went. Penn changed his tactics, began most uncharacteristically slowly, patiently.

"But look Hugh, you can't leave everything lying round your room much longer. Suppose your mother comes up."

"She never does."

"Just occasionally she does," added Jean, from where she lay apparently asleep.

"She's just as likely to be suspicious if we're up there all afternoon on a day like this."

"She's never suspicious. She never bothers to be."

"She does bother," Hugh almost shouted, then added in a lower voice, "I don't want to do it this afternoon, I tell you. I just don't want to. It is my room, isn't it?"

"So you've already said," agreed Penn. But Hugh's agitation had neatly calmed his. "All right, all right," he was saying amiably. "Not this afternoon. Tomorrow then. Who cares?"

It took Hugh a moment to realize he had won his point, and he was left bewildered, mentally unsteady. It was like pushing all your weight against a door which then opened easily, leaving you staggering.

CHAPTER SIX

Hugh lay on his back, gazing up into the sky, feeling the prickle of grasses under him. They had come to the park for the afternoon, all four of them. The girls did not usually accompany the boys but now whatever they did or did not do seemed related in some way to the cupboard – rather as a shadow belongs inextricably to the solid object from which it falls. Everything seemed necessarily to involve all of them, even when it did not actually involve the cupboard.

Anna, however, had complained of a headache after a while, somewhat whinily; a migraine she called it.

"You're always having headaches," Penn said brutally, but when Anna had set off for home in search of aspirin he had watched her across the grass till she was out of sight, a thin, small, solitary figure.

There were willow trees, four of them by an empty stream, one bent almost parallel to the ground. Penn sat astride this as if it was a horse, while Jean, a little pink in the face at having Penn all to herself, leaned against the same tree.

"Migraine is awful," Hugh heard her say, from where he lay separate. "One of the mistresses at school has migraines. She has a terrible headache and she can't see anything; just a little pin point is all she sees."

A pin point; a little pin point, Hugh thought. He was looking up into the sky. He felt – for the

vast sky was nothing to his eyes, invisible layers
of air and atmosphere – as if his vision too had
narrowed some little point, which he could not
decipher immediately, and after a while with staring up his eyes seemed to be making rings of air,
as water looks when a stone falls and ripples spread
about; except that these rings moved inward, cen-
tripetally. He moved his eyes away, sideways into
grass. The stems were magnified, juicy, huge.
When he looked up again the speck, the pin point,
was nearer – had resolved itself into a hawk, hovering; even from such a height it could, he knew,
see things move among these same grass stems. It
continued hovering with blurry wings – the
moment, held, appeared an hour. Then suddenly
it stooped, fell, but jerked itself up before reaching
earth, veered off, with slow and easy strokes.

"A kestrel," Hugh heard Jean telling Penn. But
she only knew because he, Hugh, had pointed kes-
trels out to her at other times. They had left the
willow tree and were desultorily playing cricket,
Penn solo in effect, diving, catching, exercising
himself. From where Hugh lay, if grass looked like
trees Penn looked like a giant.

Hugh, his face burning, eased himself back till
he lay partly screened by bracken. The sky looked
blue again and was cut by the little teeth of the
bracken fronds. There was a sharp, green smell,
and tickings from insects he could not see. The
cricket bat flashed in corners of his vision, but
though he searched the sky he could not see the
kestrel any more and so he shut his eyes, let his
thinking narrow to a single point; a point he had
pursued, yet avoided, all day long.

He thought of dreams; that flowed in your mind when it was freed by sleep, but always remained inside your mind, did not involve physical, breakable, bones and flesh and skin.

But this world he had been into twice had made him cold; it had made him wet, so it could not be a dream world. It had to be altogether another world, another time, like Thomas the Rhymer's fairyland, where a man lived for years while no time passed in his own world. Or else – and at thought of this Hugh contracted with fear – or else, he emerged from it after what seemed but a few days, and found that hundreds of years had gone by; so that he was a stranger, out of time.

But if it had not been a dream, the reality he had experienced had been of a different kind. It was as if everything he knew had been taken apart and then put together in a different way, in a pattern just as agreeable yet apparently wayward, because it was not the pattern in which he normally lived. He might follow it in time but it would take him time to do that; as eyes take time to adjust from light to dark.

It was a world, Hugh thought, in which animals, trees, landmarks were not just animals or trees or landmarks, but friends or enemies, or both at once. He remembered suddenly, vividly, the alder trees; which had surrounded him like friends, but then tried to hinder his going, like enemies. And the birch trees – once when Hugh looked back they had seemed peaceful, harmonious, like slender peaceful women; but the next moment they had appeared as warriors, with twigs and branches for arrows and for spears.

It all came back to Hugh now, what had happened to him last night. What dream he'd had. It was not a dream, he knew, but he did not know what else to call it. And that evening, Monday, when he found himself back in this other place, it was as if he had never been away.

Light came slowly. He was still walking through the same bleak landscape, towards the same castle, which looked farther away than ever, because now Hugh could see, between it and him, the deep folds in the country which he would have to traverse. There was one fold immediately below him. A group of willow trees stood at the centre of it, beside a little stream.

The snow was patchier than it had seemed at night and the land beneath it, tired and brown and dim, was made drearier if anything by the strengthening daylight. The light was at the same time strong yet bleak; it bleached out the castle which no longer looked as if it was made of glass. It looked more like a castle made of bone.

Hugh went downwards now, into the hollow with the willow trees. The slope cut off the castle bit by bit, until he could see only the topmost battlements, and then not even them, for the hollow, engulfing him, wiped out the landscape. There was only sky and the remains of bracken, sodden and brown and patched with coarse, greyish-looking snow. There was also the group of willow trees.

Hugh put out a hand and touched a willow tree. The bark was pitted, coarse and lined. He stroked it, feeling still more roughness than his eyes saw, and when his hand slowed it took a moment for him to realize that he had not meant to slow it; that his brain had not ordered nerve, nerve had not ordered muscle, even subconsciously. The hand had seemed to slow, stop, entirely of its own accord. It was as if it had frozen. And when he touched the tree with his other hand he found that that at once was frozen too, that he could not move either hand, that indeed he could not move at all.

His brain searched out each nerve to command each muscle. But he could not sort out one from another, work out which muscle controlled which limb. He was frozen totally.

It was then that he realized there was another traveller, a man on horseback. But he was moving, he came on – Hugh heard him for considerably longer than he saw him – the jingle of harness, the clod and thump of feet on bracken. Not only could he not turn his head to see, he found that now he could not even move his eyes. They were fixed in one focus, confined to a single plane, as if he looked out from the narrowest of windows. The man passed across it briefly, and so near that Hugh saw pieces only of man and horse, not the whole at once. He did not see the man's face, and the man entirely ignored him. The sound of his going went on for a long time afterwards.

The next thing Hugh knew was his own bed. He lay in it frozen still, uncertain still how to make any movement. He felt huge, edgeless, like a landscape in which the lines of his body formed the folds and dips and ridges. Cautiously he began testing nerves; fitting muscle to limb; moving head, hands, body, and in turn each arm and leg; rolled over in bed at last, wallowing hugely, and fell asleep with a heavy sigh.

CHAPTER SEVEN

"It's *not* plastic, it's leather," said Jean. "*Real* leather. You said we mustn't put in leather things."

"It isn't leather. It's imitation. Smell it. Leather doesn't smell like that," said Penn.

"But it looks like leather."

"It's plastic and it looks like plastic."

"What is plastic, anyway?" asked Hugh to calm the two of them. But no one really knew, when they considered it. Hugh dug up the word synthetic but that led them nowhere beyond itself. "We know it's not an animal, only chemicals of some sort," said Penn, "so at least it's safe to put it in and see."

"Look I tell you Penn, you are not to have my one and only purse, even if it is plastic. And I think it's leather anyway."

"So where's your spirit of inquiry, Jean?" asked Penn.

"There's some plastic ducks in the bathroom, we could use them instead," suggested Hugh.

"Hughie's bath toys, I suppose?"

"They're from when we were *little*,' Jean said. And it was true their mother rarely, if ever, threw anything away, let alone sorted things. Downstairs in the hall, stratified by age like rock, hung layers and layers of clothes that Jean and Hugh had worn, going back to the days before they went to school; the bulk tending to reject any current garment hung too carelessly on top of them, so that Hugh invariably went to school in a blazer that had sat on the floor all night. Jean had given up long ago, and kept her coats always in her room.

Hugh returned from the bathroom with a pair of dented and faded ducks to find that Penn, meanwhile, had seized Jean's purse after all, and flung it in the cupboard. He pushed aside the feeling that he ought to be indignant on Jean's behalf – he did not actually feel indignant at all – in his interest at what might emerge. But when they pulled open the cupboard doors they found only an oily and malodorous liquid, slightly warm and definitely unpleasant, reflecting acid colours not to be found in the room. Jean, neat-stepped, tight-lipped, straight-backed, went down to the bathroom in her turn to fetch a cloth to wipe this up; but first plucked the plastic ducks from Hugh and hurled them at Penn, who fielded with utmost nonchalance, at the same time saying rather indignantly to Hugh, "We need a scientist round here, why aren't you a scientist, Hugh?" – the kind of unhelpful remark Hugh's father more usually made to him.

Penn and Anna had brought from home a torn supermarket carrier stuffed with odds and ends; a comb with a few teeth left, a ripped and moulting Davy Crockett hat ("How about ducks now?" Jean muttered on its appearance, but Penn did not bother noticing, let alone taking offence), a fleet of matchbox cars lacking most of their paint, newspapers, handkerchiefs, a box of matches, a painted wooden horse minus two legs, a china dog, a glass mug, a tin plate, a chipped china bowl; even a toothpaste tube with a little toothpaste left; also nails, screws, bits of string and thread and wire. It looked as if Penn had chosen carefully at first, then chucked in everything that he could find.

Jean contributed a small tortoise-shell box, and she and Hugh together had brought a large mahogany box with a small brass inlay at the centre of the lid. It was Jean's idea. Hugh, feeling that he had already provided more than his fair share, had sorted out all the things he particularly cared about, painting things mostly, paints, brushes, canvasses and drawing-pads, kept unlike his clothes in impeccable order, and hidden them all in his bottom drawer, turning the clothes out on to the top of the chest.

"Mum never uses the button box," Jean said. "In this house it's me that sews buttons on."

The box had sat in the bottom drawer of a huge oak tallboy as long as Hugh could remember. When little he had sometimes played with it for hours, devising button pictures and button patterns. It gave him a sense of curious displacement touching these buttons again now – a sense of loss almost – of time perhaps, but more, of himself.

They dated generations back; there were modern plastic buttons, brass buttons, plain or with anchors on, almost all tarnished; velvet-covered buttons, the velvet mostly split and faded; smooth round pearl buttons, flat, subtler mother-of-pearl buttons; some large white buttons minutely carved. "These are bone, I think," said Hugh. "We'd better be careful." "What sort of bone?" asked Jean. "How should I know," Hugh said. "How about whalebone?" suggested Penn. "I say we don't find out," said Hugh. He and Penn looked at each other and laughed and threw punches, aimed at, but not meeting, flesh.

Hugh picked a bone button from the box. Its carvings must have needed a point of needle size; they made an intricate, geometric pattern that he thought entirely abstract at first glance. But then, as he was examining it, it was as if his eyes changed focus suddenly. The pattern shifted, jumped out at him – however hard he tried he could not blink it away again. For there was a castle; flattened, one-dimensional, but a castle nonetheless with lines indicating battlements and the dimensions of hewn stone blocks.

All the bone buttons were similar. On each a castle now came to eye. Though Hugh hunted feverishly he could not find one without. Meanwhile, the familiar clack, clink, slither of the buttons revived other familiarities. The bone buttons had always been in the box, he remembered. Even the castles were not as strange to him as he had thought initially. Recognition of memory came, then memory of knowing them. Yet he did not lose his sense of shock. Bone buttons. Castles of bone, he thought. "Just suppose they were made of human bone," said Penn.

But it was hard to tell of what many things were made. The Davy Crockett hat, for instance, could have been rabbit or cat or even nylon. "It's certainly never seen a racoon," said Hugh. They were very careful at first, trying only the most obvious materials. A box of matches became a small fir tree with its roots still full of earth. ("What a pity it isn't Christmas," Jean said, but it was an uneven tree, much bushier on one side than the other.

Hugh would never have chosen it from a shop.) A brass button emerged from the cupboard as two small pieces of rock, one greyish, one yellower, that Hugh explained held zinc and copper ore before metal had been smelted out of stone.

"Man ain't this educational," said Penn. "But not just educational," Anna said quietly. And it was not indeed. You did not, in merely acquiring knowledge, wait with such a shiver between question and answer. You did not impose ritual, such as they imposed on themselves at first. Someone would advance alone, place an object on a shelf and close the door, the gentleness or firmness of that depending on who it was; Penn for instance decisive, Jean brisk, yet a little hesitant. Anna was quite as decisive as Penn, Hugh thought, but in a very different way; slower, more deliberate, prolonging each moment and giving it weight. He himself tried to shut the doors so quietly that there was no click at all. Silence in this seemed to him aesthetically necessary, even satisfying.

Then they would wait; silent and intent. Light in these moments took on almost the quality of sound for Hugh, while sound had a grainy texture to his ears, as if he could touch and see, as well as hear it. Sometimes, waiting, he felt no tension. Sometimes, for no apparent reason, with no apparent difference the tension was unbearable. He noticed Anna watching him once. He had been scratching his groin, only half consciously, and hastily he moved his hand. The movement broke the thread, for him, for everyone. Someone opened the cupboard door. This time a white cotton handkerchief had turned into a plant with a fluffy untidy head.

"Everything has stages of development," Penn said. "But we don't know which stage the cupboard is going to choose. It takes things back to any stage, you can never predict what."

"Hugh's wallet turned back into a pig itself. His sweater didn't become a sheep," said Jean.

"If you put a person in," said Anna smiling at Hugh, "a person of thirty, say, they would come out a baby or a child, or even a younger grown-up. And you wouldn't know which in advance."

"That's exactly it." Hugh felt Penn watching him smile back at Anna.

"That's exactly what I meant. How about trying a person then," Penn said. "You would do fine, Hugh." He nudged Hugh, a nudge perhaps sharper than necessary. Hugh might have protested or retaliated had not the cupboard at that moment illustrated the point exactly, by returning for the chewed and twisted toothpaste tube, instead of a heap of materials, a new tube, shiny, plump and full. It might have come straight from the manufacturers.

All of them suddenly became lit and warm and wild. They rolled about with laughter, as if someone had made a particularly funny joke. But the excitement was dangerous, frosty-edged, a little hysterical. The tortoise-shell box became actually a tortoise with blinking eyes and a prehistoric scaly skin – the first live creature to emerge from the cupboard since the white sow itself – which so fired Penn that he grabbed Hugh's one silk scarf from an open drawer, and let the cupboard turn it into a silkworm, little as a pin. None of them could find this at first, it was so small, and while they hunted on hands and knees, Jean, enraged about the scarf and still angry about her purse, seized, from the back pocket of his jeans, Penn's diary, in which he put the dates of his cricket and football games. It emerged from the cupboard an unattractive mixture of wood-pulp and oil. "So *that* wasn't leather-covered either, Penn," she said. Hugh thought Penn might actually hit Jean then. He towered; his fist was raised, his face on fire.

From then on they seemed to be arguing all the time. Penn accused Jean of being officious; Jean accused Penn of bossiness. Hugh was distracted, felt apart and unhelpful, succeeded only in being clumsy. Anna said almost nothing but carried on exactly in her own way. She irrationally but quite profoundly irritated Hugh, who dismissed the feeling as one of the many he had these days which seemed much too large and unwieldy for whatever had aroused it.

Ritual first blurred, then entirely disappeared. They started to shove everything into the cupboard at once. Newspapers and buttons, string and nails emerged in pointless, unpromising heaps, from which it would have been impossible to disentangle the origins of anything. As Hugh raked out the whole lot rather angrily on to the bedroom floor, his sister Jean turned uncharacteristically perhaps the wildest of them all, rushed away downstairs, returning a little later with raisins, dried beans, a box of salt, and a jar of meat extract with a bull's head on its label. "Well you can ditch that for a start," said Penn.

Hugh took the raisins from her hands. They were actually muscatels, in a three-cornered box, very wrinkled and dried up. He put them into the cupboard and closed the door on them just as his mother walked in, panting a little from the climb up four flights of stairs.

She stood in the doorway shouting. She wore a brown cotton skirt with a split in one seam and the hem halfway down the same side. Her hair must have been newly washed the way it flew out from her head, with a blur of little lights round the edge of it. She never had the smooth, the polished look, that Hugh thought other people's mothers had.

And there they were: Hugh standing by the cupboard, with his hand on the catch; Jean, flushed and unusually rakish and untidy-looking, holding a box of best sea salt; Penn leaning nonchalantly against the window, his body distorting a beam of light; Anna sitting on Hugh's unmade bed, holding the little fir-tree from which she plucked needles and crushed them between her fingers – Hugh's nose caught wafts of their small strong pungencies. His mother looked oddly at Anna, looked at her twice, but did not speak, as if she could not quite analyse why what she saw was strange. Then she swept across the room and pulled open the cupboard door.

"Grapes, *Grapes*."

"I bought them," Hugh said hastily.

"Come buy," said Penn, "all fresh, all sweet."

"Who'll buy . . ." Jean's voice started on a high note, split, fell into helpless giggles. They were particularly lush, fat, purple grapes, lying on a heap

of wood shavings. Hugh's mother ate three before
letting fly at Hugh again.

How could he have had the cupboard since
Sunday (Saturday, muttered Hugh) and not put
anything away in it? How could he have such a
mess in his room? What were grapes of all things
doing in his cupboard? (she ate another three). As
she went on Hugh's anger mounted, was beginning to match hers, until he saw Penn giggling
ostentatiously behind her back, then he turned his
anger, bent it against Penn, let most evaporate in
a single glare.

But when, her rage faltering, she had gone, they
all fell on and devoured the bunch of grapes. And
all, including Hugh, lay round the floor giggling
hysterically.

"You must admit it's a problem," Penn said
finally.

"What problem?" asked Hugh, suspiciously.

"To have a cupboard you can't use as a cupboard. If you put all your clothes away as your
mother said, you'd be nude; you wouldn't be
decent to go in the street. So what are you going
to do? She's bound to come back again." They
all collapsed once more at the thought of Hugh's
nakedness.

"Oh I'll hide them; stuff them away somewhere
and keep the cupboard shut; then she won't know
it's empty."

"You can't get away with it for ever," said Jean.

"Well we'd better make some effort to tidy
now." Penn climbed to his feet, brushing himself
down. "No more cupboard, not for now. All

hands to clearing up the place. Get up, Anna, you lazy little beast."

Anna had been lying under the window on her back, with her eyes closed. She did not stir at first when Penn poked her with his foot. Then slowly and deliberately she opened her eyes wide, and a moment later raised herself on an elbow. She must have been lying on that hand. Its skin had taken on the ridges of the worn cord carpet.

"Get up, lazybones," said Penn. "Get up and help."

Anna giggled. "It's not my room. I'm not going to."

"You are, you know."

"I'm not, you know."

"You jolly well something *are*." Penn grabbed her under the armpits and began to heave. She left him all her weight and annoyed, he grew rougher, dragging her. "You're *hurting*," Anna said.

"Get up then."

"No." Anna laughed again.

"*Get* up," Penn shook her furiously. She stopped laughing abruptly, set her feet down, wriggled round, lashed out, fought with him, Penn's greater strength quite matched by her fury.

"She was hurting, really scratching," Jean said to Hugh afterwards. "And kicking. Did you see? I've never kicked you like that, or scratched."

"Well he was brutish enough too. But you wouldn't call her timid exactly. I always used to think her timid. She scarcely opened her mouth at all."

"But she is still timid, in a funny sort of way," said Jean.

The fight had stopped as suddenly as it began. Anna froze, looking at Penn's watch. "Oh Lord, oh dear, it's after one already. I promised Mummy I'd be home to help with lunch." She seemed all anxiety and awkwardness, and left without picking up a thing.

Penn bellowed down the stairway after her. "When we try putting a human in the cupboard, it'll be you, Anna, you'll be the guinea-pig, if you don't damn well watch out."

CHAPTER EIGHT

Hugh gazing out of his window after lunch saw Penn and Anna turn out of their gate and up the road. He spent a great deal of time gazing out of his window. It amused and occupied him at least when he had nothing else to do or when a painting was going badly, and at most it left him with an extraordinary, strange, creative ache; a beautiful yet unbearable sense of growing out of himself, exploding skin and bone. He tried to catch this feeling sometimes, record it, pin it down. But always at once it faded, or collapsed like a blown-up paper bag.

It gave him a pleasing sense of power too, gazing out of his window. He felt god-like – seeing people who did not see him, scratch themselves, or mutter or gesture dramatically, unaware of being watched, people with whom he had no need to involve him-self, as merely passing in the street he would have had to be involved. Like a god he felt above time even, anticipating event. He knew for instance now, that the car nipping so busily along the road was about to be brought up short behind a trail of cars barred by an oil-delivery tank; and again seeing a poodle shut up in a parked car, a large alsatian approaching on a lead foretold an enjoyable eruption of which no one else was yet aware.

Anna and Penn were just ahead of the dog, walk-ing slowly, their heads together. Whatever did they always have to say to each other, Hugh wondered, with annoyance. In company Anna was so silent usually and Penn critical of her or teasing.

The poodle sprang against its window barking furiously. The alsatian leaped explosively, thunderously, almost dragged its startled owner down. Penn and Anna jumped apart, Anna scuttling in at the gate, Penn almost scuttling too, but then pausing and shaking himself and walking in with dignity, while Hugh laughed himself silly in strangely malicious triumph and amusement.

"I saw it coming a mile off," he explained.

"I saw it too," said Penn aggressively.

"Rubbish," said Anna, "neither of us did."

"Well are you ready, Hugh, anyway?" Penn asked.

They were going to the Royal Tournament, a military display; not a function Hugh would have chosen for himself or indeed any of them, except Penn just possibly.

"It's hardly for pacifists," Hugh commented.

"Well I'm not a pacifist. Why? Are you?"

"I'm thinking of it. I was last term."

"I bet you're not. Rubbish. It's just affectation."

Penn's father had been given four tickets by some business acquaintance. "It's free entertainment, isn't it?" Penn said. "It won't entertain me in the slightest," protested Hugh, and indeed when he walked into the exhibition hall that afternoon and saw tanks and guns lined up, the array of dowdy yet lethal armaments, he almost retreated and went home at once.

He resisted everything at first; the marching, the patterns made by the marchers on the arena floor; the sound patterns made by the armorial bands.

He felt that disliking the belligerence for which
these stood, he ought not to allow shivers to run
up and down his back. Yet he could not have come
to an event more suited to his, to all their present
states of mind, because of the noise and glare and
ritual; and though he did not want to be carried
away and lost, soon fell into a state of dream which
came dangerously near to it.

Looking down on the arena, an oval of orange
sand, Hugh felt above time again, anticipating
event; except that here, the formations moving,
advancing against each other, he would have antici-
pated collision rather than their actual neat enfold-
ing, row on row, each rank sliding whole through
others and emerging whole. The lights changed
ceaselessly. The troops were all green one moment,
then white, then pink, then scarlet, then all colours
together at once. The lights and music jointly hyp-
notized him. By the time the gun race started –
two teams of sailors from different naval ports
dragging guns and gun-carriages over an obstacle
course – he was yelling like everyone else and
totally overcome. And when it ended, with a crash
of cannons and a cloud of bitter smoke which
touched their faces and hung pale against the darkness overhead, as against a tangible, solid surface,
the pleasure he felt was out of proportion to the
event. He seemed to explode with light and relief
and joy.

"Well, I think we can say that went off with a
bang, ladies and gentlemen," said the voice of the
avuncular colonel in the commentator's box. Penn
and Hugh looked at each other derisively, shrieked
with irreverent laughter. They leaned across Jean

and Anna who were sitting between them and shook hands solemnly.

"What an absolutely *sooper* bang," they said all but simultaneously, with exaggerated army accents. Just as Hugh came out of cinema feeling bold or reflective or poetical, according to the film, so now he took his mood from the tournament. He felt splendid suddenly, glittering, a match for Penn any day, using words for weapons, flinging them along the row, across both Jean and Anna. "Don't mind us," said Jean indignantly. And twice, somebody behind Hugh leaned over and tapped his shoulder, and told him, authoritatively, to keep still, be quiet.

"And now," proclaimed the relentless jolly colonel, "we offer you a dangerous and stunning event. Every week, ladies and gentlemen, these brave teams suffer a broken bone or two, practising on your behalf, to entertain you now. We present to you, proudly, on motor-cycles, the Army Daredevils!"

The stadium suddenly went black. The sour smell of horse urine drifted up from the arena floor. People waited, rustled, coughed a little. A roaring grew from somewhere – lights went up suddenly – it was as if that made sound as well as light, for the noise grew furious, the great doors flew away, with a roar and a rush in dashed a chain of motor-cycles – two, three chains, one behind the other; black motor-cycles, black-clad riders. They roared to the far end of the arena and back again, split, wheeled round and rode diagonally across each other, missing by hairs'-breadths, then returned

with mighty, restrengthening roars. Even sceptical
Hugh held his breath anxiously.

"Want some more, gentlemen?" inquired the
colonel.

"No," yelled Hugh and Penn together, and
looked at each other grinning. "They'll crash,
they'll crash," Jean was saying frantically. "Oh I
wish they'd stop." But Anna seemed to like it as
much as Hugh and Penn. She gripped the seat, her
face open, full of life.

"You haven't seen anything *yet*," bellowed the
commentator. "Now for a mid-air crossover," –
and then in a moment, when it was over – "Want
it again?" he asked.

"Oh I hate it, they'll crash," wailed Jean, as the
motor-cycles dashed once more on their opposite
diagonals, rode up ramps and jumped, missing
others by inches in mid-air.

"*Miss*," whispered Penn. "Come on, *miss*,"
whispered Hugh, and heard an echo, it must have
been Anna, sighing, "Miss . . . miss . . . miss."

Jean watched no more, just turned miserably
away. When the cyclists, having crashed through
walls and leapt through hoops of fire, departed at
last, leaving an obtrusive silence and petrol fumes,
her relief broke out in furious irritation.

"I'm sick of you leaning all over me, Hugh. If
you and Penn have to be so stupid, why don't you
just sit together. I'll move up."

She shuffled along into Hugh's place while he
climbed over her. But there was still a space on
her other side. Anna simply had not moved at all.
Hugh looked at her, puzzled, and waited for her.

"Budge up, Anna, there's a love," he said to her at last.

"Budge up, Ann," hissed Penn more urgently. A new event was expected in the lit arena. From behind came murmurings, protests, as people shifted and craned their heads.

"Sit down, will you," ordered a louder voice, behind.

Hugh, desperate, climbed over Anna as much as it was possible, Penn beyond having squeezed up as far as he could. They earned more disapproving glares from Penn's other neighbour, but Anna still had not moved at all. Since the motor-cycles went a light might have gone out in her. She gazed straight ahead, expressionless. Hugh sat down firmly, anyway, partly on Anna, partly on Penn, which was effectively uncomfortable for Anna shifted, only fractionally, but enough for him to fit, just, into the space between her and Penn. Her eyes never strayed from the arena once. She sat very straight and held hands demurely with herself, her left thumb tucked inside her right fist, the fingers folded on top of it. Hugh noticed a tell-tale chewing movement in her cheek.

Then at last he looked back to the arena. And saw what, despite newly added props, had been there all the time. And yet he had not consciously taken it in. It was as if till now he had not been allowed to take it in; it was as if, just as with the button box, his eyes had refocused, slightly shifted vision. He saw a castle, another castle.

He leaned over the still unyielding Anna and snatching the programme they had bought from Jean, leafed through pages of advertisements to find the table of events. "Event Number Twelve. The Attack," it said. "The siege and storming of an English Castle. A re-enactment of medieval warfare, staged and presented by Colonel Bassett-Brown M.C."

Hugh returned the programme to the indignant Jean, and looked back into the arena; at what his eyes, his mind and something less obvious had contrived to keep from his consciousness. There was a crudely painted castle on the end arena wall, around and above the entrance doors. It was two-dimensional, apart from turrets on either side, battlements which jutted a little way into the arena and a drawbridge across a simulated moat. Three-dimensional, it would, however, have been a square castle.

The teams of men working in the arena fell into line now, and in line ran off. The light changed, dramatized itself. To the sound of trumpets an army entered from the opposite end of the arena, headed by a man on a black horse bearing a standard. His armour was silver, but his flag, shield and tunic were a dark holly green with scarlet devices on them. Archers appeared on the castle battlements. The drawbridge was lifted. The invaders brought scaling ladders and a battering ram. The attack on the castle began.

Hugh never doubted that the attack would succeed, and could not remember subsequently a single detail; only the curious relief he felt when the castle had been stormed and taken. ("It isn't a patch on Ivanhoe," Penn whispered in his ear. "Now that *was* a proper castle.") He did not understand why its capture should seem so crucial, nor why he should feel such relief, since he already knew the outcome. Yet he did feel relief. It carried him through the rest of the programme in a dream, scarcely noticing any of it, his ears still filled with the triumph of trumpets, his eyes with the glitter and fierceness of steel points and blades. The castle was flat again, amateurishly painted, yet still to his mind and memory it was stone, four-square and strong against invasion and attack, the picture in his mind more powerful than the one before his eyes.

He dreamed that night; indeed he not only expected, he forced this dream, or had the illusion that he did. He felt all-powerful. He took the holly trees along the fence in their garden, rearranged them in his mind, and sure enough found himself beside a line of holly trees on a hilltop, looking down on the castle now, or so it seemed.

He was close enough to see it in more detail than before. Trees stood near it, leafless still, and the wind blew mightily and threw the trees about. It looked almost as if the castle standing among them turned, spun, as if it revolved on a spool or plinth. There were bushes as well as trees crouched close to the ground like animals – like lions, Hugh thought. Some were bolt upright, some lay flat, yet all were wakeful, watchful. The roaring of the wind sounded like the lions roaring. The whole landscape seemed to have come to life about Hugh today.

And then he saw a man below him galloping towards the castle. It was the man he had seen before, but there was a glitter about him now. Bit, bridle, sword and spear gave off little points of light. Hugh thought he heard sounds from them, clinks, glitters and jinglings, just as he had thought he heard the roaring lions.

Horse and man galloped in slow motion at first, uphill, but they quickened rapidly, the slope levelling out. As they swept faster and faster across the ground, Hugh began running too, stumbling over the prickly grass, while the castle turned in front of him. He thought he saw men on the battlements now, archers with bent bows. He could have sworn there were roaring lions all around – watching the castle instead of his step, as he gasped for breath, he lost footing, stumbled and fell, banging his head severely. He lay with the sky, the earth, the whole world spinning and turning about, then within, his head, then found himself lying giddily, in darkness, in warmth, in his own bed.

He stilled the spinning deliberately, by turning between the sheets. Something prickled him through his pyjamas. He put his hand down and the same something was prickling his hand, several places at once across one small area of skin. He pulled out a holly leaf, and threw it on the floor beside his bed.

CHAPTER NINE

Next morning Hugh provided the forgotten tortoise with a cardboard box and some lettuce leaves. Then he set up an experiment. He had woken with a passionate desire for knowledge; not simply to watch the cupboard working as they had done yesterday, but to understand the mechanics, how and why it worked. Just as he always wanted to paint alone, so now he wanted to do this alone. He peered over the bannister on their landing to make sure that Jean was not on her way upstairs, and then closed the door very quietly and carefully.

The box of buttons was beneath his bed. Hugh pulled it out, opened and searched through it carefully until he found three brass buttons, all identical except that one was less tarnished than the other two. This one Hugh chose to put in the cupboard first, shutting the door on it. He timed the interval by the second hand on his watch and after thirty seconds exactly, opened the cupboard again.

The second button he left for a minute on the same shelf; the third for one minute and twenty seconds. The first button emerged like the button the day before, two lumps of rock veined just decipherably with metal. The second was still a button, but infinitely shinier, as if new from the maker's mould. The third button, left in longest, came out smelted, liquid, hot. Hugh burnt his fingers and swore out loud as the metal cooled and hardened before his eyes.

Rummaging in the button box he managed to

find a fourth brass button, with an anchor on it, just as the others had. He left this in for the same length of time as he had the third, but it emerged only as two lumps of stone, like the button he had left for half a minute only.

He concluded then that you could not control this past at all; that is, you could not determine the stage of its past to which you wanted some object to revert, by the length of time you left it in the cupboard. The cupboard worked to its own timings, had its own logic. It would have comforted Hugh a little to have disproved that, if only minimally. If time as he knew it, running in a straight line, from the past through the present to the future, had related to the cupboard, even in reverse, it would have been something to cling to, to make him feel safe. It must be orthodox time, he thought, which made life seem relatively stable and ordinary. If time melted, had no force, then space, the whole physical world would easily melt as well. Hugh longed for one aspect of the cupboard to be controllable.

He stood staring at it, as if the cupboard itself, its wood, its form, might divulge some of its reason and purposes. He held a door open with one hand and rested his other hand on a shelf. He was stretched across the cupboard, his arms wide, but the cupboard seemed to hold him, rather than he it. The sun flowed past him, bringing out the close grain of the wood (so close that to the naked eye it scarcely made patterns on the wood, as coarser graining does). Light brought out the differential tarnishing of the thin brass hanging-rail. In one place he could see all colours there, oilish rainbow colours like the colours of the melted plastic.

Hugh dropped his hands suddenly and stepped right back. He clenched his hands and stood perfectly still, his head singing curiously. He took one step forward – hesitated – pulled his foot back.

He wanted – he could not look at what he wanted, because he knew that he must not, should not do it. But he wanted to; only, he was afraid. He put his foot forward again; he could not help it, it might have been dragged; and snatched it back. And again he could not help it, for his fear took over. He felt the two contrary pulls that he had felt before, himself ruling neither, yet ruled by both. They cancelled one another now and left him motionless.

He wanted to get inside the cupboard. There was a little, clear, moving picture inside his head, of stepping in, crushing himself up, pulling the doors shut on him. The doors snapped across his mind, cutting off pictures, making his eyes blind. It was dark inside the cupboard. The brass rail sang above him. He could see nothing now, only feel it.

Darkness. Hugh shook his head. For there was no darkness, only full daylight, hot sun. He stood staring at the cupboard, and the wanting to enter it was still so strong, it pulled him forward. He took one step forward and another, telling himself it was only to retrieve the pool of hardened metal that still lay on the floor in front of the cupboard. He bent, reached out a hand, stepped forward again. One foot was actually in the cupboard now.

In a moment the rest of him would have followed.
But –

"Hugh, *Hugh*," came a voice behind him and
the crash of an opening door. "Penn and Anna are
here. Mum says we ought to go. She'll take us
down to the station."

"I don't believe she's ready, for a start." Hugh's
voice belonged to someone else. His eyes blinked
in the sunlight.

"Well she is, for once. You'd better hurry up,"
said Jean.

"Well I'm not."

"Well hurry up. What have you been doing,
Hugh?"

"It's far too late to go anyway. It'll be jammed
by now, in the holidays. I haven't been doing anything."

They were going to the zoo. It was one of
Hugh's favourite places, he went there often, by
himself. He went to observe and also draw, animals, buildings, people – observing perhaps quite
as much if not more than he actually drew, keeping
all forms, animate or inanimate, in his head, playing around with them, distorting, rethinking them,
and setting them on paper at last, if ever he did,
transformed by his feelings and impressions; forms
both remembered and remade.

These expeditions, however, were not only
strictly solitary but usually as early in the morning
as the zoo opened. He had been planning this trip
alone too – attracted as much as repelled by the
prospect of the crowds, because he had meant to
observe them as closely as he observed the animals
– but his mother had seized on it as a means of

paying back yesterday's hospitality by Penn's parents. (Penn's mother had given them all supper after the tournament.) Hugh had protested of course, but less than he would have done ordinarily, because his wish to be solitary had been partly overlaid by the compulsion to be with the other three. He had no choice in any case, the matter was decided by his mother, which for once made things easier. She gave Hugh money for all of them and a picnic lunch, rather untidily wrapped. She also gave him three letters to post, because she said she would like them to have the zoo postmark on.

Penn had been angry about the zoo at first; he considered it childish. But he could offer no better suggestion, and when it came to it, all four being in a curiously dreamlike state that day, the zoo seemed as good a place to dream as anywhere. Even the ordinary animals seemed creatures of fantasy, and the stranger ones had never appeared so extraordinary; elongations, distortions, incredibilities; long-necked giraffes and long-nosed elephants, loose-limbed gibbons swinging hand over hand from rail to rail to rail, seals sliding into and through the water, smooth-skinned, rubbery (they barked and splashed, but the movements were unrelated, entirely silent); striped tigers; and lions, *lions*, thought Hugh, and pushed the thought of lions away, deliberately.

He went to the elephant house. House felt the wrong word though, it was more like being underground in an eccentrically lit and hewn-out cave, or like the crypt of a castle (Hugh wished he could stop thinking of castles, too.) There were staged areas of orange light, in which, framed by pillars, wrinkled, primaeval-looking creatures stood, elephants and rhinoceroses, their every wrinkle having definition and importance. Hugh felt as if he had never properly looked at either animal before. They were dusted most of them with yellow sand, this thicker in the cracks and wrinkles, and looked more like reptiles than animals with their naked skins and little, sunken eyes. They looked like that pig, Hugh thought, and again wished that he had not.

He stood and stared at one rhinoceros, bigger than the rest; it stared back with surprisingly mild-looking eyes, almost benevolent.

"Wouldn't like him for breakfast," a girl said behind Hugh and giggled. Hugh did not turn around, but glowered to himself.

There was a trench between animals and onlookers, a shallow trench with steps down into it and short stone blocks lining the centre, like old-fashioned milestones. It was scarcely a barrier. He and the rhinoceros might have been in the same dimension, there seemed nothing to stop Hugh reaching it, or it reaching him. It felt familiar suddenly, and then Hugh realized that it was like standing on the hill looking across at the castle. As then, he seemed close and yet remote. When there came sudden movement, he even expected it to be a man on horseback, but it was only a little girl who ran down from the viewing floor and clutched at one of the stone blocks in the trench. Hugh gasped, moved to snatch her from danger, his sense of alarm heightened by what he had been imagining. But no one else seemed to think it dangerous.

A man walked down the steps and brought the child back on his shoulders, smiling, while behind him the rhinoceros ambled to the rear of its enclosure. It moved joint by joint as if made by an armourer. Its skin looked as if laid on it in plates, by nails. It did not look real at all, Hugh thought. Perhaps what seemed ordinary reality was no less odd than his new world after all, just as the new world could come to seem as ordinary as reality.

The other three waited outside the house.

"We've had enough of this. Let's eat in the park," said Penn.

"We could row on the lake then, afterwards," said Hugh, glad at the thought of escape, "I've got enough money left."

"The letters," Jean said. "Will you post them, Hugh?"

Hugh stood staring at the letters, blinking furiously, his eyes taking an inordinate time to adjust themselves to daylight.

"What's the matter?" asked Penn, echoed by Jean. All of them were staring at him oddly, Hugh thought. He glanced around wildly, he wanted to escape, but he could not; anywhere he turned he saw them, castles. The elephant house, the bear terraces, the seal rocks all looked rugged, turreted, like castles with battlements and towers.

He held up each of the letters in turn. There had been a new issue of stamps only yesterday. Hugh had never seen these before. One letter bore a stamp to go to America, another a fivepenny, the third a threepenny stamp. The theme was the castles of England: the first had Carmarthen Castle, the second Windsor, the third, Harlech Castle.

"Castles," Hugh said to himself, and then out loud "Castles." He managed to shift himself and set off running through the crowds to find the postbox at the main gate. He could not get rid of the letters fast enough, they felt like fires in his hand, imagined or real he could not judge by now. He went to the wrong gate, and so could not find the postbox at first, dodging frantically through the milling and purposeless crowd, mistaking a woman in red for the box once, and finding it at last more by luck than decision, throwing the letters in immediately. One missed the slot, it dropped, he had to pick it up again. And when it was done, when all three were gone, he leaned against the box, gasping, to the surprise of the postman who came at that moment to empty it.

"You all right, mate? You a student then? You've got the student look."

Hugh shook his head, and walked away soberly. His panic worked through him; slowly cooled, uncoiled itself. He took in the ordinary zoo for almost the first time that day, the sour smells of animal and chip fat and DDT: how hot it was and how hopelessly crowded. There were queues for everything, lavatories, snackbars, camel rides. Thousands of children in their best clothes ran around freely, but increasingly fractious, while animals prowled behind bars or ditches, or lay stretched, panting, in the heat of the sun.

CHAPTER TEN

Anna and Hugh shared one boat; Jean and Penn another. Anna very slowly and deliberately climbed into a boat with Hugh, Penn visibly annoyed by this, Jean upset because Penn was annoyed at having to share with her. Her way of demonstrating it was to be sharp and bossy, organizing her face into a smile sometimes, but wasting it only on the water.

Penn demonstrated his annoyance by showing off wildly. He climbed to his feet, stood on the thwart, balancing precariously. Jean stopped smiling altogether, said "Don't, Penn", anxiously, first on his account and then on her own, as the boat swayed dangerously.

The boatman bellowed at them from his landing stage, threatening to fetch them in at once. Everyone rowing on the lake, the people walking along the shore, turned to look at them, making Jean blush scarlet. Penn muttered rudely, nothing that the boatman could have heard, sat down and began to row with furious but quite elegant efficiency, making the boat shoot through the water. He kept his eye triumphantly on Hugh struggling more clumsily at his oars behind, but though Hugh glanced round occasionally and coolly admired Penn's skill, Anna ignored him, trailed her hand in the water, turned her eyes towards the sky. She smiled at Hugh when he looked her way, but he tried not to do it often. He liked to cut himself off mentally from everyone around him, usually

annoying people thus, but he could not now quite
cut himself off from Anna, which at this moment
only annoyed him. He avoided her eyes. She was
holding hands with herself again, and she wore as
usual a dark-coloured dress. But today it did not
overshadow her.

Penn rowed so much faster that they lost him
soon, round an island in the lake. Hugh rowed on
towards the island. The branches of weeping
willow brushed his face and shoulders like bead
curtaining. He pushed them gently out of his way.
He had stopped rowing now, but the impetus of
movement already gained took them as far as he
wanted, between the other branches and the shores
of the island. They slid through still water and
came to a halt within a green cave.

Anna appeared to be asleep now. Hugh looked
at her, then gingerly, carefully, laid himself back.
The position he came to might, indeed should,
have been uncomfortable, but was not so at all.
He seemed automatically, without experiment, to
have found a position into which every part of
him neatly fitted, rested comfortably. He lay in
contentment, gazing at a green ceiling. His hands
and face were green-tinted, Anna's too, but green
differentially. Here and there pure sun fell through
the willow fronds. Hugh was so comfortable now
that he could forget specific bones, specific physical
sensations. He and the shade and the tree and the
sun were all one and the same, all melting together.
It was a cool, detached, thinking place, Hugh felt
– the words "Green thought in a green shade"
came from somewhere, he did not know where.
He could think green, cool thoughts about castles;

about the castle, about the cupboard, green, calm thoughts, compared to his panic that morning. It was as if he had fought in a vast wind then, but now the wind had died. He found himself contented, not at all afraid.

Anna sat up. Hugh felt her first in the rocking of the boat, and when he sat up himself found her gazing over the side of it. The water was very green and thick, her reflection green and remote and strange. She stirred the water with her finger, the image of her face shivered, disappeared, came together, her hand pausing, then disappeared again. The small ebbs of water caught points of light that Hugh would not have known existed in this shade.

Hugh wanted to reach if not Anna herself, the image of Anna. Beyond, infinitely deep, as the water shivered and before it settled he seemed to see another image, of a castle, and he wanted to reach that too. He realized he wanted to think of it, to be reminded of it. He wanted terribly to reach it. But the water stilled, the castle was not there.

"The water's filthy," Anna said.

"It's a beautiful colour," Hugh said.

"It looks like soup. It ought to smell horrible."

"But it doesn't," Hugh said.

"It doesn't smell nice, either."

There was further silence. Hugh had no inclination to break it, but after a few minutes Anna said: "I was thinking about the cupboard; your cupboard."

"Just for once I wasn't," Hugh said.

"What do you think, when you do think?"

"How should I know now?" Hugh did not want to commit himself.

"You must know!"

"Nothing useful, anyway." But suddenly Hugh did want to tell Anna about the castle, everything. It was as if a space had opened in him, revealed something he did not know was there. The wanting sprang at him from nothing, but the desire fought inability, he could not tell her, could not find the means, words framed themselves only to split upon his tongue. She did not seem to want to be told in any case. Every time he thought he had gathered himself to speak she ran her fingers roughly through the water, or shook her head, or turned abruptly, or said something herself about ducks, the tree, the zoo, always something trivial, if not downright silly or at least it might have been downright silly, or she might have deliberately calculated silliness. Hugh would not have put that past her. Eventually he told her just about his experiments that morning, timing the brass buttons, though he missed out his wanting to get into the cupboard.

Anna was silent when he finished. Hugh watched her reflection in the water with almost the same curious nostalgia he had felt for the girl in the alder grove; both girl and reflection thankfully unobtainable.

"Would your old man be able to explain us anything?" asked Anna startling him. "The one in the shop, you said."

"We could try I suppose."

"Then go and ask him. If you want to know."

"Do you want to know? But what do I say. Er

um did you know you sold me a magic cupboard, sir?"

"That's *your* problem not mine," said Anna calmly. "Now listen, if someone got into the cupboard, they might be made younger, mightn't they, just like Penn said?"

"We thought of that yesterday."

"I thought of it, you mean." But Hugh wanted to think about this even less than he had wanted to think about the old man, because of what had happened this morning.

"Anyone old could get into the cupboard and be made young again. They could grow old again and be made young again. They needn't ever die."

"I suppose they wouldn't. But think of the practical problems."

"They would be immortal," Anna said.

"An odd sort of immortality. Gods are immortal, but they always stay the same. They don't ever get old, get young again."

"I'd hate that," Anna said. "I mean I'd like to be immortal if I could go on changing. But I think I'd have to go on changing."

"Some Indian religions say you change totally. After death you come back to life as an animal, insect, anything. I read that once."

"That's silly. You know it's not what I meant."

"I'd be a bird, I think, if I was allowed to choose."

"I'd be a squirrel or a monkey. I'd like to leap and swing, like those gibbons in the zoo."

"That's flying too, of a sort," Hugh said. "Would you really want to be made young, Anna, over and over again, to keep changing and never die?"

"I change anyway. I change every day, don't you? I feel years older than Jean. Sometimes I feel years older than you." Anna was laughing at him suddenly.

"You surprise me. Anyone would think you were Methuselah. You look ancient, I must say, Anna. Come off it, for heaven's sake."

"Come off what?" asked another voice. It was Penn this time, holding aside the trailing branches, letting in a swathe of light and sun, a view of the world outside. Hugh did not want it, world or light or Penn. He felt a sudden total fury. But Penn stood in the bows of his boat like a figurehead, triumphant, all his ill-humour gone; perhaps it had been transferred to Jean, who looked, behind him, red-faced and annoyed.

"He won't let me row, Hugh. He hasn't let me row at all."

Penn laughed at her. "She is entirely in my power. If she snatches at the oars she'll just upset the boat."

"Hugh, he's horrible, it isn't fair. Can't I come with you, you'd let me row."

"Willingly," Hugh answered lazily. It was as if a switch had flicked, his fury gone utterly, he could not remember what it felt like. "I hate rowing myself." But he found when he came to it that he was less happy to relinquish his companion. He would rather have rowed with Anna or with Penn than Jean, who moved into his boat clumsily, not rocking it too much, but still much less neat than

Anna, who smiled gently as she sat herself down in Penn's boat.

Their hour was almost up. Penn rowed off at full speed, widening the gap between their boats at every stroke. Anna sat in the stern with her back to Hugh and Jean. Her voice and Penn's floated across the water, but Hugh could not hear anything that was said. Jean's rowing was perfectly adequate, but she kept up a running commentary on the techniques involved, that he did not feel in the least like listening to. She fell silent at last out of weariness; but Hugh did not offer to take over the oars. Aware, without guilt, that he was being mean, he lay with his hands behind his head and simply enjoyed himself again, let the sun, the slight wind, the cool movement of water calm him, just as he had been calmed earlier in the willow grove.

CHAPTER ELEVEN

They went home as they had come, by bus and underground. In the tunnels, in the dark, the distances seemed interminable if you once began to count. But when the train broke out into the light, when the eye had something it could reckon by, even twice the distance might seem half the length. So time always was in part what you made of it, Hugh thought, a little comforted. It made the cupboard seem a shade less ruthless, a shade less arbitrary.

They walked in at the front gate, hot and cross after the walk from the station.

"Where's Humbert?" Jean asked at once. Humbert was the cat, Jean's in effect, because no one else took much notice of him, except, occasionally, their father who fondled him extravagantly before visitors, or when he felt some kind of need to show affection. In the summer, in the heat, Humbert's favourite place was beneath the ash tree in the front garden – he had been sitting there when they went out, but was not on their return.

"He'll be somewhere. He could be anywhere. You know what cats are like."

It was odd that Jean worried so very soon. But when they did begin to look for him he was nowhere to be found. His dish of food had not been touched either.

Jean was beside herself. She seemed at the moment too easily upset, who was normally quite calm and organized. She went all round the house, all round the garden, calling quietly, "Puss, puss, puss." To no avail; by bedtime she was crying unashamedly.

"We shouldn't have gone out. We shouldn't have left him. It's all our fault."

"Don't be silly; Ma was here." And they'd often left him, Hugh pointed out, gently. He'd often gone off and then come back. Cats were like that, independent, solitary. "I'm dead sympathetic to cats," Hugh said with feeling; remembering he'd hardly been left alone to paint for a week, and wishing, almost, that the cupboard had never happened.

He went upstairs to bed still thinking of painting, not thinking about the cupboard at all. But there had been a tree in his most recent painting, somewhat abstract but a tree for all that, dominating it, and it was a tree he began to feel as he neared his room; an ash tree, he decided, because that was where they'd last seen the cat. He expected the cupboard to be a tree, to have taken root, to be growing in his room. He opened the door quite sure of that, to find only the ordinary shoddy-looking cupboard, marked by nails where there had been a mirror, and the ash tree as usual outside his window. Yet he had imagined an ash tree in his room, with a smooth trunk and sprays of little leaves.

His mind kept on going back to it. Lying in bed he found himself in a boat, floating beneath the shade of a huge ash tree. Tonight he felt wholly as if in a dream. A boatman stood in the bows of the boat and poled it with a long grey pole. Hugh could not see the boatman's face but this did not worry him – he seemed to know everything, some-where in his mind.

The castle lay ahead of them across the lake. Hugh looked for and found its reflection in the water, but under the lake he saw another world again, the castle surrounded by flowing grass and trees, trees with fruit on them and some with flowers, all greenish-tinged, all the other colours there but subordinate. Hugh longed for the castle, stretched out his hands to its reflection, the boat gentling and gliding under him. His hands touched the water, stirring it, and ripples came and broke the world. Then he awoke to lie quite calm and peaceful, his body, released, almost floating in the bed. He did not need to move to make himself comfortable. He fell asleep like that and did not dream, and woke in the morning lying as before, not a limb having shifted, not a finger.

It was very early, well before breakfast. Hugh got up and went to the park and walked by himself in clear, cool sunlight; shadows important, light significant. Sight and sound were quite separate experiences – the roads were full of cars, but the noise they made was not all related to the engines that made them. It was a calm, a whole, yet dis-jointed world, empty of anyone save Hugh him-self. The people in cars were part of the machines, and so did not count, he thought, as people.

He walked for much longer than he meant and came back late even for his mother's breakfast, meeting Penn and Anna at the gate. Both looked cross, appeared to be arguing – they stopped when Hugh arrived and smiled at him, but the smiles might have been to spite each other rather than welcome him, he thought.

The house smelt of sausages and shaving soap, among other familiar things harder to define, because they were always there, and well amalgamated. But as they went down the basement stairs, another smell met them, strong, unpleasant, all too recognizable.

"Cat," said Penn, disapprovingly.

"But our cat . . ." said Hugh.

"Perhaps Humbert's come back," Anna said.

But there was in the kitchen no full-grown Humbert, only a black kitten regarding gingerly a saucerful of milk. On the other side of the saucer Jean knelt, looking at the kitten.

"He's sweet," she said. "He was sitting outside the cat door, just as if he wanted to come in."

"He's peed. It stinks," Penn said.

"Perhaps we could keep him even if Humbert does come back. He looks a bit like Humbert . . ."

"Black all over," Anna said.

The moment he had seen the kitten Hugh knew what had happened; what the kitten was. Anna knew too. He looked at her quickly, found her looking at him – both hastily removed their eyes from each other. Anna scratched her nose and chewed her tongue, and seemed not particularly concerned. Hugh, decidedly shaken, looked at the table and considered unenthusiastically a cold sausage and two elderly slices of toast.

"Is that my breakfast? Where's Ma?"

"Upstairs, cross, gone to get you out of bed."

"I've been for a walk. God almighty, we usually have to get *her* up," said Hugh indignantly.

"She was in that sort of mood this morning. You know, energetic."

"For once," said Hugh.

"Your ma *energetic*?" Penn asked.

"Shut up," said Hugh furiously. "It's none of your business."

"Isn't your room still in a mess?" asked Jean.

The kitten was actually lapping now; lapping milk slowly, with deliberation.

"Humbert," Hugh said. And felt Anna nod.

"We can't call him Humbert. Humbert might come back. It's still only one night after all."

"He won't come back," said Hugh, but to himself.

Anna paused when they started up the stairs, waiting for Hugh who was scavenging for food.

"Do you remember what we said yesterday?" Hugh ate the end of a sausage and considered the question. He could see Penn looking down at them with some hostility.

"Immortality," hissed Anna eagerly.

"I don't think much of an immortal cat," said Hugh.

"The Egyptians thought cats were immortal, sacred anyway. We've got a postcard on our mantelpiece."

"What are you talking about. What's got into you, Ann?" shouted Penn from the top of the basement stairs.

"Nothing, except my brother," Anna said coldly.

They met Hugh's mother in the hall, still in her dressing-gown and very indignant. All the time she was shouting she looked at Hugh's toast and marmalade, as if wondering whether to eat a slice of it herself.

"Why can't you have your breakfast at the same time as everyone else?"

"There isn't a time in this house . . . Just because you woke up for once . . ."

She let it pass. It was his room she was really concerned about, working herself up into a greater and greater rage as she went along, having started relatively calm. She stood in the middle of the stairs, blocking the way up – Penn tried to dodge past her, but without seeming to notice she moved when he did, so preventing him.

Anna was giggling, a silly schoolgirl giggle, at Penn, annoying him, at Hugh's mother, annoying and confusing Hugh, who did not know which of them to turn on first, his mother for attacking him, or Anna for attacking his mother. His anger mounting, though undirected, he scarcely took in anything that was said, knew only that the abuse was centred on his room, its chaos. On the empty, apparently unused cupboard.

Shock was delayed when it came. Hugh heard the words clearly, but did not take them in. It was like this morning, seeing an action at a distance and hearing it fractionally later, except that this time it was the other way about. The sound came first; seconds later arrived the blow.

Penn's mouth was open. Hugh at first could not imagine why. Then he saw that Anna's expression was curious too, amused, perhaps triumphant, and yet alarmed.

Since Hugh had been so slow to put his clothes

away, well she had done it for him, his mother had said.

"*Jesus,*" said Hugh those seconds later, diving past her, up the stairs. His mother's voice floated angrily after him, but he scarcely heard it, tearing breathlessly up the red-carpeted stairs, his step never matching the tread or two treads he was trying to take – too long, too short, his pace disjointed, the very fall of his feet knocking the breath from him. His mind seemed to burst with the dangers and possibilities.

"You won't have any clothes left for a start." Penn behind Hugh did not sound even out of breath. Anna appeared to be laughing; Jean puzzled, frightened, uncomprehending. "What's happened, someone tell me?" she went on and on, all the way upstairs, more and more breathlessly.

But when Hugh at last flung open the bedroom door there was nothing. The room looked much as he had left it earlier, his pyjamas on the floor, his bed unmade. The only difference was that some of the untidy piles of clothes had been removed from the chest-of-drawers and placed in still untidier piles on the cupboard shelves. But clothes they remained and nothing else. For his mother, typically, had failed to shut the door. Pants, vests and shirts, were still pants, vests and shirts, not collections of miscellaneous materials, or blunderous frightened animals.

Hugh and Penn collapsed simultaneously, laughing, and rolled together across the floor, punching each other, laughing again and punching again, to the ribs or face or chest, punches not serious, scarcely felt, shadow-boxing like young animals.

But when they stopped, as suddenly as they had begun, climbing to their feet, dusting each other down, Hugh saw Anna by the window, unsmiling.

"Come on, better get this lot cleared up a bit," said Penn officiously. "Come on, Anna, get moving, girl."

But she did not move. She did not seem to hear. For the first time Hugh began to take it in, the atmosphere here, in the room.

Outside, the clarity and glitter of the early morning had vanished. The sky had not so much clouded over as thickened to a grey haze, not dark but sullen, emphasizing the heaviness of late summer foliage, its lack of bloom and life. Hugh imagined autumn with relief.

But it was more than that. Outside the ash tree blocked the window and there was a constant procession of holiday aircraft, flying low because of the haze, the haze itself trapping the roar of their engines, bringing it right into the room, thunderous, oppressive, heavy. Yet the centre of the power that oppressed Hugh so utterly came from within the room itself. It came from the cupboard; engulfing, enormous and quite impersonal, so that Penn's efficient activity taking clothes from shelves and hangers seemed merely busy and insignificant. The black kitten strolling into the room, its tail pointing to the ceiling, looked more important, curiously. Yet it was ridiculously small.

Jean fell on the kitten with relief, but it twisted from her hands and settled calmly by the window, with all the assurance and indifference of an adult cat.

"I wonder where Humbert is," said Jean.

"This is Humbert."

"A kitten. Don't be idiotic, Ann."

"It *can't* be Humbert." Jean did not even want to believe it.

"It is Humbert, isn't it, Hugh? Hugh and I talked about it yesterday. This sort of thing."

"Why didn't you talk to me?" asked Penn.

"You wouldn't have listened. You're pig-headed, Penn. You tell him, Hugh."

Hugh reluctantly tried to explain. But it was difficult, Penn intrigued but not wanting to believe out of pride and Jean not wanting to believe out of fear. Anna's self-righteous look made Hugh wish he could disbelieve it himself, but in the face of the black kitten's presence, and the mysterious and unprecedented absence of the black Humbert, the explanation did seem all too probable.

"He must have got into the cupboard while we were out yesterday."

"But how could he have shut the door?"

"Well that is a bit odd, I know," admitted Hugh, but it did not affect his certainty.

"It turned other things back, didn't it?" Anna pressed; the harder it was to disbelieve her, the angrier Penn grew.

"We'll have to shove you in to make sure, Ann."

"Oh no *you*, Penn. You were such a sweet little boy, everybody said."

"Well you looked like the back end of a bus. So everybody said."

"You were so pretty, you looked just like a girl."

The angrier Penn got, the sillier the insults; Hugh had hardly seen him so angry before. He started throwing clothes on to the bed, furiously, as if they were weapons. His anger made him powerful, almost as powerful as the cupboard itself, but the fury appeared to bounce off Anna. She stood calmly watching him in the middle of the room.

"I can show you. Ma has those photographs of when you were little. I'll show you the one of Penn without any clothes on, Hugh. He looked sweet." Anna's voice rose. "Suppose we put him in the cupboard and he came out like that?"

Hugh and Jean might have been in a different world. Watching Penn and watching Anna, Hugh felt wholly remote from them. He could look away, and it would not be happening. It was like a picture flickering on a screen that you could turn off with a switch. Only there was no switch, and he could not look away, and it went on happening.

"You'd be much much nicer, Penn. I could cuddle you."

Anna was no longer cool, but laughing, a little hysterically. And when Penn, the cupboard emptied, turned on her, lashing out blindly, she took the excuse to lose her temper too. Penn lashing out, she jumped at him. Penn stepped back from her, and taken off balance lurched, stepped back again, swayed awkwardly and fell into the cupboard. It was almost as if, voluntarily, he folded himself up in it, because Anna was able to slam the doors on him – Hugh would have expected the furious Penn to push them open instantly but he did not. The cupboard remained shut.

It was so sudden. First this had not happened, then it had. Anna covered her face, looking small, thin, childish. She took her hands away and stared helplessly at Hugh, horrified, yet dazed as if she had suddenly woken from a sleep. She stood alone beside the cupboard door, but it was Hugh who took the four long, creaking steps across the room and opened it, noticing as he did so his sister Jean, mouth open, eyes open, totally startled, almost a caricature of surprise, like someone drawn in a comic strip.

He stood, holding open the cupboard door. His eyes descended. Looking at first for the boy Penn, his vision had to adjust itself to the proper scale, to find at last no Penn he knew, but a baby in T-shirt and dungarees, with reddish curly hair, holding a brass button out to him, and smiling unconcernedly.

He was so nice, that was the trouble. For it only made this still more horrible.

CHAPTER TWELVE

"It can't be Penn. It can't be." Jean's voice shook miserably. The baby waved his arms up and down, giggled, and crawled out of the cupboard.

Hugh dragged his mind back, tried to force the presence of this baby towards the earlier presence of Penn, to make himself understand properly that this could be Penn.

"Who else could it be." He spoke as much to convince himself.

"We must put him back in the cupboard quickly. Quickly."

"Don't be stupid. What good would that do?" Hugh felt weary; a lethargy came over him at the thought of trying to resolve this. At the thought that he had to; Penn having left him to decide alone.

A wave of furious anger came over him as well; that Penn should have so abandoned him. He touched a chair, could have thrown it across the room, but the anger faded, left him void and cold.

"What are we going to do?" he said.

"Look after him, obviously." The immediate and pressing practical problems began to have the effect of calming Jean. When the baby, crawling for a chair, almost pulled it down upon his head and began to wail, she moved quickly, picked him up, cuddled him, murmuring.

"Shut him up *quick*," Hugh said. "Or Ma will hear."

"What if she does come?"

"We'll hear her. We'll have to hide him fast."

"Hide a *baby*. Are you *joking*?"

"She mustn't know."

"But someone's bound to notice Penn's missing, some time."

The baby was quiet now, patting at Jean's cheek. Jean shifted her face to one side of him to look at Anna. Hugh looked too, almost simultaneously. Anna was standing quite still, her arms by her sides, with hands curled up, shaking all over. Her eyes were shut, tears were spilling out and pouring down her cheeks.

"Anna," Hugh said, questioningly. "Anna?"

She opened her eyes and looked at him.

"It's done now. It's happened. I think," he said cautiously, "it would have happened some time anyway." But the tears continued pouring down Anna's face.

"You will have to pull yourself together, Anna," said Jean officiously, forgetting her earlier panic. The baby was pulling at her hair now.

"Tonight's all right," she added. "Penn and Anna are meant to be staying with us tonight anyway or they could if they wanted to, Mum said. Their mother's going out. But . . ." Hugh made a helpless, hopeless gesture. Anna merely began to weep out loud. Hugh wanted to go away now, do nothing, seek no solutions, but pulled himself out of that, through irritation mostly.

"Shut *up*, Jean. It's all right, Anna."

"It isn't all right. How can we get him *back*?" Anna's voice wailed somewhat, but at least she began to look more normal. For an unpleasant

moment Hugh had wondered if she might be going
to faint; she had looked so ashen white.

"I don't know, not yet. We'll think of something. But I don't know, *yet*."

The baby had started whimpering. Jean looked
helpless again. "Do you suppose he's hungry?" She
jigged him up and down, but to little avail. Anna
walked across the room and looked into the baby's
face as it peered over Jean's shoulder.

"He *is* Penn. He looks like Penn." The baby
stopped whimpering and stared at her for a long
time, solemnly. Then suddenly he smiled, while
Anna smiled back. Hugh had never seen her smile
like that before. It was a nice smile apart from
anything else, and he realized he did not always
like Anna very much, that is he did not always
think her nice.

Both Anna and Jean seemed after a little while to
become more concerned by the immediate problems of child-minding than by anything else. Hugh
envied them.

"How old do you suppose he is?"

"Fourteen months? Sixteen?" Jean hazarded.

"What do babies of sixteen months eat, then?"

"Chopped things."

"Liver, I remember," said Anna. "Oh and
mince. My aunt gave her baby mince once, I saw."

"But not raw mince. And we can't cook. Not
without questions."

"How long is he going to stay like this? For
goodness *sake*," Anna sounded frantic again, but
this was a point that none of them cared to contem-
plate for the moment, and Jean suggested hastily,

"There are always those little jars. You know the ones."

"Yes, but those are for little *tiny* babies."

"There are some for bigger babies too. Chopped things."

"Well give him those then." Hugh was bored of the discussion by now. "And meantime keep an eye on him. An eye . . ." He made a dive. The infant had started wriggling frantically. He was heavy enough, hard enough to hold without that, so Jean had been forced to set him down, and in the discussion they had all forgotten him. Now Hugh saw him put the flex of the record player in his mouth. "Jesus, he'll kill himself," he said. But the flex taken away from him, Penn howled and struggled in Hugh's unpractised arms.

"Shut him *up*, Hugh. Everyone will hear. For goodness *sake*."

"Shut him up yourself if you're so clever. Look, we'll have to get a room organized for him. Your room's better," Hugh added hastily.

"My room isn't so lethal. It had better be mine. I'll clear it up with Anna. You can get the baby food, Hugh."

"I can do *what*?" Hugh was appalled. "I haven't any money . . ." Then, realizing it was a chance to escape, if only for a short while, added, "I dare say I could raise some."

Outside the house the ordinariness of things was astonishing. But then so was the far from ordinary way in which Hugh found himself observing them. It felt like coming out of an exhibition of modern paintings and seeing the familiar world through the eyes of the artist, quite different eyes from his own.

.

Or it felt like looking through a mirror, seeing familiar things in a dimension from which he was alien; quite cut off.

The racks of baby food in the chemist's shop were another alien world – an unfamiliar one anyway. Hugh had never noticed them much before, but now nothing might have existed for him but the possibilities of beef with tomatoes or veal with rice or lamb with vegetables, all sealed in jars with coloured labels on.

"Can I help you?" a voice asked loudly. Hugh jumped, and also, to his annoyance, blushed slightly. "I want some of these," he said, and blurted – to his annoyance once again – "for my younger brother."

"I never thought it was for you. Well, take your time then. Looking's free, unlike most things." The assistant was very young, but Hugh did not look long enough to know much more than that, whether she was as pretty as she was impertinent. Annoyed with both her and himself, he became decisive, took a jar of spaghetti with beef, another of vegetables with lamb, a third of pears with apple; but a fourth – chocolate custard – he had to replace hastily, realizing he had enough money only for three. That cleaned him out, as it was, for the rest of the week. Hugh hoped Jean had some money, or Anna, whose brother after all was causing the expense, and wondered disconsolately again how long this could possibly go on.

A very old man came into the shop just as Hugh was leaving it, and asked for cough lozenges. His voice was like the shadow of a voice, the frail centre, from which the rest, the resonance, had been honed away. His clothes hung as on a frame. His face was suspended between two great ears and a jutting nose; two noses would have seemed appropriate for total symmetry. Hugh, half out of the shop already, stopped still and stared at him.

At first he thought: I'd rather die before I become as old as that. And then he wondered: what would the old man have looked like young, and then what would happen to him if he was put into the cupboard. Would he be made young also? Or could someone be too old for the cupboard to change them? And how much younger would he be made if the cupboard did work? A middle-aged man – a young man – a baby? The thought of him as a baby was bizarre – or bizarre looked at conventionally. But Hugh could feel normality slipping away, the fixed world melting about him. Who would look after him if he became a baby? He would not be claimed by anyone, his real parents must have died generations ago. Would you wrap him in newspaper and leave him on a doorstep, like the cases reported in the evening newspapers? Or would you be able at once to find someone who wanted a baby to adopt? All these dilemmas merged in Hugh's mind after a while and moved it on to other questions; concerning another old man, the old man in the junk shop. What had the cupboard to do with him? Was it merely in his shop by chance? The thoughts kept galloping through his head, he could not tell how long they lasted. But the old man was putting the lozenges in his pocket as the assistant said, "Did they never tell you it's rude to stare. Perhaps you've a little sister too, how about buying her some baby soap?"

"No thank you," said Hugh. He walked out of the shop very slowly and deliberately. Then he ran all the way home, clutching to his chest the bag full of baby food, and bumped into his mother at the front gate.

"I've got to go out. I told Jean," she said. "There's cheese and eggs when you want lunch. Oh and yogurt."

"There's always yogurt," said Hugh. "The last lot went bad."

"And salad. You can make a salad."

"Where are you going?" asked Hugh. He had too much on his mind to be much interested. But he felt he had a right to know.

She did not answer. At once he wanted to know very much.

"Where are you going?" he insisted. She looked at him this time. But all she said was; "Penn and Anna can stay if they want."

"Why don't you ever listen," said Hugh, "When I ask you anything?"

"And of course they may be staying tonight in any case. Penn and Anna, Hugh."

"I wasn't asking about them."

"Why shouldn't they stay to lunch too? There's plenty of yogurt."

"They'd better like yogurt." The baby might eat it, Hugh thought. That meant they could save the jar of apples and pears till tomorrow. Tomorrow. His mind tried to shy away from that word, but only came back to it. Tomorrow and tomorrow and tomorrow ran through his mind. They had been reading Macbeth at school last term. Macbeth's problems, he thought bitterly, had nothing whatever on his, murder was *nothing* by comparison with this.

Then it dawned on him that with his mother gone, they would be safe for a while at least. It was very odd, he thought, that it had taken him all this time to realize it. Now he was impatient for her to go. He saw her look down at his hands, at the bag of baby foods, carried half open, carelessly. But she did not seem to take in its contents and he closed it hastily.

"You might wash up. I'll be back by three. I'm only shopping."

Four, with luck, that meant, thought Hugh. She leant forward suddenly, might have been about to kiss him, but withdrew. There was a hole in the armpit of her shirt. She went straight off and up the road.

"Why are you buying *baby* food?" she called back suddenly, but did not wait for an answer. Hugh felt almost faint with shock. He dropped the bag and had to pick it up again. The glass jars, fortunately, remained intact.

Upstairs Hugh felt quite outside of things. The girls' fussing over Penn excluded him; he did not know whether he cared or not, decided probably not. Jean's room had been turned effectively into a nursery. She had improvised a cot with the mattress that was kept jammed under her bed and had been for years, and which was brought out whenever she or Hugh had friends to stay. Indeed either Penn or Anna would have slept on it tonight. But now she had put it in a corner and fenced it around with chairs. "I shouldn't think he could get out of that," she said. She had also found a whole lot of toys somewhere, mostly very battered.

"Isn't it a good thing your mother doesn't throw things away," Anna observed.

"The garden shed's just full of marvellous things," said Jean enthusiastically – she had even unearthed an ancient pushchair. Hugh had to help the girls set it up; it had been folded so long it was reluctant to unfold at all, its joints seemed set, its parts inseparable. Nor were they assisted by having the infant Penn crawling about their feet, and by the kitten which had elected to appear from the basement, pleased with itself for some reason, purring loudly, and insinuating itself among them, until Hugh trod on a paw by accident, whereupon it miauled indignantly and retired to a safer distance.

Eventually, the three of them pulling as hard as they could, the pushchair unfolded, clicked into shape. It was a little drunken-looking perhaps, and decidedly rusty; but a usable pushchair for all that.

"Penn could have done that on his own. He's strong enough," said Anna.

"Well Penn's not here, is he?" said Hugh, unkindly.

"Why do you want the pushchair?" he suddenly inquired, "Surely you're not going to take him out?"

"No one will know who he is," said Jean. "We'll just say we're obliging someone, looking after him."

"You're *mad*," said Hugh. "We don't know anyone with kids that age."

"If we just take him in the garden there'll be questions anyway," said Jean.

"If we take him out," said Anna, "he's more likely to get to sleep."

The baby fell asleep after they had fed it, much to their relief. It was only then they realized how anxious he made them. It was a bit like living with an unexploded bomb, Hugh thought; they snatched their lunch like people between air-raids. Even Jean did not bother to organize them for once – it was Hugh and Anna boiled the eggs and washed the lettuce, while she stayed upstairs minding the baby. They ate the lettuce straight out of the colander with the boiled eggs and chunks of bread and butter and almost a packet of sultanas between them; it was better than yogurt, Hugh thought. Certainly better than the glutinous orange mess from the baby food jar – Penn had not cared much for that either, judging by the amount he'd spat out, with a delighted smile; they'd had to feed him cheese in the end. Jean said she was sure cheese was bad for babies, but Anna retorted that it was better than leaving him to wail with hunger, so announcing his presence to the world.

Hugh left the house on his own after lunch before Penn had woken, not saying that he was going, let alone where. He thought: they wouldn't be interested anyway. They were only interested in Penn. He was halfway up the road before he knew where he was going himself, and then again he did not know if he had decided it himself or whether it had been decided for him. Either way there was no doubt. It was where he had to go.

He went down the hill, back to the junk shop,

pushed the door and went straight inside. The smell and the dim light were immediately wholly familiar. But when his eyes had accustomed themselves to the gloom, he saw that something else was different, more, very very different. He ought to have known why immediately. But it was as if he had seen the shop in a dream before; he could not visualize, merely summon up a feeling of what it had been like. Not until he deliberately stopped himself trying to remember and let impressions sweep over him unimpeded, did he realize what had happened. The shop was emptier, not just a little, much emptier. The furniture was still there, or a fair amount of it, blocks and forms and shadowy shapes, but most of the clutter had vanished from the surfaces and nothing hung from the ceiling now. There had been no tables outside the shop either, Hugh remembered suddenly, no boxes of books and junk and jewellery, and piles of 78–speed gramophone records. He wondered what had happened to everything. It could not, surely, have been sold in just a week.

The shock was as great as the first time; of coming from light into shadow, from warmth into chill. First he noticed the difference, then at last he placed it, the relative emptiness, then he saw the blind head – on a table now, in a corner and without its wig; and then he saw the old man looming from a doorway.

"I was only looking," Hugh said, apologetically.

"Looking's free," observed the old man: at which Hugh, instantly, from nothing, wanted to laugh, an emotion puzzling to him, almost embar-

rassing, and quite inappropriate in these circumstances; but the pert girl in the chemist's had said
exactly the same thing, and it seemed so out of
place here, like a dirty limerick spoken in the
school chapel. He stared at the old man defiantly.
"I'll go on looking then," he said.

His eyes had adapted to the dimness now. He
saw a single object on every single piece of furniture, or on a wall above, a whole range of objects,
each one as separate and distinct, as before they
had been indistinguishable amid the general clutter;
yet each one at the same time related to all the
others, though how he could not say. There was
the familiar yet still disconcerting blind head.
There was a squat stone figure of a monk; an
eighteenth-century miniature, a wooden oval disc
with a face carved on it in relief – it should, he
guessed, have hung upon a wall, but now lay face
upwards on a marble stand – and another wooden
head, more jutting and ornate, which might have
been one of a pair supporting a doorhead or a
mantelpiece. There was a group of pottery figures,
a sailor, a girl, a curly-tailed dog, all brightly
painted so far as in this gloom it was possible to
tell; a medallion very tarnished which looked old
– was it Roman? Hugh wondered. It had a face on
it too, and so did the small chipped saucer on the
table next to it, a formal portrait head. On the wall
above these, equidistant from both, hung a little
print of a man on horseback, etched or engraved,
brown-spotted with damp.

Everything, every object had a face, Hugh
realized, the same face, one he half recognized,
but could not place. The looking, however, so

absorbed him that the voice from the inner doorway made him jump uncomfortably.

"You came with your father before, young
man."

Hugh turned towards the voice, the shadowed
face. "We bought a cupboard. Yes," he said.

"Ah yes. I remember it; a cupboard with qualities."

"Some qualities," Hugh said. "It was a very
ugly cupboard too." For a moment he only
remembered the ugliness of the cupboard, and
nothing else at all.

"You may call it ugly if you like."

"It *is* ugly. It's why I came. I came about your
cupboard." Hugh spoke quietly. He had thought
he would have to force himself to be calm, but it
was not difficult at all. He felt calm and controlled
and certain what he meant; at the same time cut
off, separate from everything. "Your cupboard
changes things," he said.

"It's your cupboard, not mine. You bought it
from me. Or your father did. It is his cupboard I
should have thought. What did you expect? What
was I supposed to offer you? Continuity? Security?
Immunity? Immunity from what?"

"I don't know what you're talking about. If you
buy a cupboard you don't expect it to change
things. That's all." The words were protesting
enough, but Hugh, feeling it entirely absurd that
he had to protest at all, could not put much heat
into his voice. All at once the whole thing seemed
ridiculous. He was himself ridiculous. "It changes
people," he said trying to retrieve the seriousness
of the situation, and yet somehow not able at this

moment to feel serious enough, in spite of everything.

He wondered, suddenly, what Anna would have
thought.

"It's not so unusual for people to change," said
the old man, prim as a governess.

"Not like that they don't. What's it made of?"
Hugh managed to sound a little more insistent; yet
still, inappropriately, wanted to laugh.

"What would you have liked it to be made of?
Gingerbread?" asked the old man. But now he
turned and led Hugh out of the shop into his little
back room, flicking a switch as he went, so that
they passed from dimness to light again – which
made Hugh blink uncomfortably. There was a bare
bulb swinging idly on a long flex, throwing
shadows of itself upon the walls. There was a table
with papers on it, an unlit gas fire, an electric
kettle, but, surprisingly, not a single chair or stool.
The old man's face had turned to islands and
shadows now.

"You should have warned us," Hugh said.
"Why didn't you warn us?"

"Would you rather it had not changed things?
You could have bought some other cupboard.
Cupboards are not in short supply."

"It was the only cupboard in your shop,
though," said Hugh. He avoided answering the
real question. But the answer came rushing at him
even so, and he resented this answer, because the
cupboard had been, to say the least of it, inconvenient, upsetting everything he had meant to do,
destroying his solitude, stopping his painting,

imposing impossible problems on him, and leaving him to solve them without Penn, alone.

"I might be glad in a way," he said angrily, then laughed out loud. "It's all right for Penn. He can't notice anything, he doesn't have to do anything. He just has to be looked after. Jesus, I wish it had happened to me, not Penn."

"But you are not Penn," the old man said. "What you have to do is different."

"Then you do know about it?" But the old man looked at him and shook his head very slightly. They stood in silence for a while. "What's the cupboard made of?" Hugh asked. The old man went past him back into the shop and fetched a chair, but neither of them sat down on it. They continued to stand beneath the naked, swinging bulb, which went on swinging for reasons of its own, making little reflections of the room and them.

"What shall we do? How can we get Penn back?"

"The cupboard is made of apple wood," said the old man slowly and deliberately.

"A mighty big apple tree to make a cupboard. And so what? It's wood like any other wood."

"Not *an* apple tree. It need not have been a cupboard either."

"What's so special about an *apple tree?*"

"*The* apple tree. Aren't you an educated boy? What does it signify?"

"I don't know, I don't care. But what about the other trees?"

"Alder," asked the old man, "and birch?" "And willow and holly," said Hugh. "And ash . . ." He waited. The old man finished it. "And oak and apple. Would you rather it had been an ordinary cupboard?" he went on.

"I don't know. Why should I tell you?"

"Then why should you expect me to answer your questions? The shop is closed. Didn't you see the notice? You are taking up my time and there is not much left of that, if you choose to destroy it as I fear you will."

"The door was open. I don't understand what you're saying."

"The sign said closed," insisted the old man. Hugh saw this sign now out of the corner of his eye, the old man edging him backwards, through the shop. Indubitably, it did say closed, in large black letters. The door was open and Hugh outside.

"I must have forgotten to lock it," the old man said and smiled and locked the door in his face and pulled down a blind, leaving Hugh foolish, baffled and uncomfortable, alone in the cobbled street.

CHAPTER THIRTEEN

Hugh took the longest way home possible: first along the river, by the crowded towpath, then around the green, through the town and past the station. He walked abstractedly, his eyes to the ground, sometimes kicking at it resentfully. The world beat outside him, but he was no part of it; when he bumped into people their glares and rebukes at once both alarmed and failed to touch him, to mean anything. He scarcely looked up or bothered to apologize, just dawdled on moodily, pushing out his lower lip, a habit he had when sulking, or rather he had used to have, for he had mostly grown out of this by now.

The crowds thinned out as Hugh left the shopping street. Walking up Chapel Road over the railway bridge he met scarcely anyone at all.

He paused there. He leaned on its painted steel wall, rested his head upon his hands and gazed at the other world, the railway, below him. There were no trains now. Before him reached an expanse, a prairie of shining steel, the criss-crossing of parallels an almost illusionary perspective reaching as far as he could see. It bore no relation to the journeys it provided for, juddering along in hot and dirty trains, brought to his mind rather the image of another illusionary perspective, in the dream, not-dream, he'd had last night; the expanse of shining water in the centre of which stood the castle he had to reach, surrounded by fruit trees. The word Avalon slid into his mind, suddenly; he did not know where it came from. But before he could start trying to remember, a voice said behind him.

"Hugh. Hugh." He had not heard a car draw up; he almost jumped out of his skin, turning to find a familiar white but rather grubby Renault behind him. Out of it leaned Penn's mother.

Hugh made his face as blank as he could.

"Do you want a lift, Hugh?" she asked. There was nothing he wanted less, least of all from her, but his mind was beyond finding credible excuse, even if he had the energy to use it. For it would have needed energy to refuse her. Her kind of forcefulness carried everyone along.

"Are you thinking of painting it?" she asked. Hugh stared at her in bewilderment. "Paint what?" he asked, thinking of the castle. "You were such miles away," she said.

She was, on the face of it, the reverse of Hugh's mother, thin, dark and quick, with a pointedness about her, and an impression, almost, of glitter. The kind of clothes she wore, and made her daughter wear (always in or beyond whatever fashion happened to be, or else, triumphantly, scorning it) which quenched Anna, seemed to set her alight. Today she wore a tight black T-shirt, white jeans, and on her head, tied gypsy fashion, a black and white silk headscarf; glitter was provided by long jet earrings which swung when she moved her head.

She looked like a bird, Hugh thought; a magpie perhaps, she was so very insistent, so very black and white. He remembered with relief, and laughed to himself that his father always called her

Birdfeet. His own big, slow, fairish mother, it suddenly occurred to him, looked much more likely to be the mother of the large red-headed Penn than Penn's mother did herself.

"Hop in," she said leaning over and opening the car door. When Hugh continued to gaze at her, unmoving, she patted the seat. "Get in. Get in," she urged again, her head slightly inclined, one eyebrow raised, asking questions without pronouncing them.

He attempted to arm himself, mentally, against her; sat on the edge of the seat, praying for the journey to be over quickly. "Shut the door," she told him. For he had not shut it completely; he might, deliberately, have left himself a means of escape. It was always the same with Penn's mother. He never knew whether he liked her or not. For one thing she always seemed much more interested in his painting than his own mother ever was, indeed far more interested than in the athletic achievements of her own son, Penn. ("What that means is having to stand for *hours, freezing*, on the edge of some muddy field. They're all so covered in mud I can never tell which Penn *is*," she had said to Hugh's mother in his hearing, though he'd never heard of her actually going to watch Penn take part in any game.) But she did not show her interest in Hugh by asking questions. She was much more tactful (or subtle) than that. She broke down his guard by saying nothing, or by looking at him inquiringly, or by seeming amused or impressed, changing each attitude as he fathomed it for another; so that he never knew quite where he was, whether she was laughing at him or taking him seriously. Yet he felt that unlike most people he knew, unlike his mother, she understood sometimes what he was trying to say. Sometimes this exhilarated him. At other times he resented it very much; he did not want anyone getting inside his head. Almost always when he saw her advancing on him he attempted to escape, and if he could not, deliberately put up his guard, resisted her interest, calling her Birdfeet in his head to put her in her place. But almost always before he realized, she'd broken down his guard again.

Today his preoccupations were beyond anything even she could guess he thought, with a slight sense of triumph, feeling her glance at him, enquiringly, as they drove on up the hill. She did not fail to notice the total panic which suffused him upon her turning the car into their own road.

"Calm *down*, Hugh," she said as he stiffened and peered through the windscreen ahead of them. "I don't know what's the matter, what's biting you, I won't ask, it's none of my business. Just don't take it so seriously, that's all. It can't be *that* bad."

That's what you think; just for once you're wrong, thought Hugh. At that moment he saw precisely what he feared; turning into the road from the far end, Jean, Anna and the pushchair advanced, inexorably towards them.

They stopped abruptly at the sight of the car. Hugh saw them look at each other, in horror no doubt, though he was too far off to see their expressions. He saw Anna say something to Jean. She must have suggested that boldness was the only course, because they set off again and advanced towards them steadily, arriving at

Hugh's front gate just as the white Renault drew up at the kerb besides it.

Would Penn's mother recognize him? Hugh wondered, detachedly. How could she not recognize him? On the other hand how could she, without making that giant mental step into the belief that such things were possible; that her teenage son could be returned to childhood in such a way. He realized how far he himself had come now to believing in such things; he'd had to. Penn's mother didn't have to though, he realized suddenly. Not unless he, Hugh, insisted that she did, and even then she might still not be convinced, might end up thinking him crazy. He wished he could convince her. That way she'd have to take charge of the whole matter, so relieving him.

"Get a move on, Hugh," her voice was urging him. "Unless you want to stay the night in the car, that is. It's all the same to me."

Even so she leaned over and opened the door for him, and stayed leaning once he'd got out, staring at the baby.

"Where did you manage to steal him, Anna? Not from outside Sainsbury's, I hope?"

"Of course not," said Anna primly. "He's the brother of someone at my school." The answer must have been previously prepared, it came out so neatly, so directly. Jean more hurried, less convincing, added:

"We said we'd look after him – so she could go out shopping."

"We've only got him for a *little* while," said Anna.

"So I should hope." But her mother spoke some-what abstractedly, without her usual bite.

She still leaned uncomfortably across the front seat of the car, regarding intently the baby Penn who ignored her, absorbed in playing with the buckle of the pushchair belt. Even her earrings were motionless, save for the minutest flicker of light on one, which came and went without apparent cause. There was also a movement of light on the side of the car. Hugh after puzzling realized it was made by the movement of Penn's hands and the glitter of the steel buckle reflected there.

"We did think he looked a bit like those pictures of Penn as a baby," said Anna, her face completely blank. Both Hugh and Jean gasped, audibly, both stared at her. Her mother sat up abruptly. "Don't be *silly*, Anna. His hair's a bit like, that's all. I'm not sure Penn's wasn't lighter too. You are obsessed with Penn, that's your trouble. You think *everyone* looks like Penn." She pushed the seat down and fished around in the back of the car for various packages and paper bags.

"Take some of those for me, please, Hugh. Incidentally," she added, reappearing, "incidentally where *is* Penn?"

"Oh he just went off somewhere," Hugh said hurriedly, "I'm not sure where."

"You know Penn," said Anna, coolly.

"I thought I did." She was briskly gathering more parcels and handing them to Hugh, who in confusion bent to help and only succeeded in banging heads with her.

"Oh *leave* it," she said in an irritated voice. "Just

shut the door for me. Have you locked it? Lock it then.''

She dropped one of her paper bags while locking the door on her own side. It had Brooke Bond Tea written on it in blue letters. The two half-pound blocks of butter that fell out declared themselves to be especially imported in similar blue letters.

"Where are you taking him?" she shouted after Jean and Anna, retreating as fast as they could up Jean's garden path. "Aren't you going to take him *home* again?"

The baby peered round the edge of the pushchair and grinned at her. Again she stared at him and again looked away.

"All babies look alike," she said to Hugh, angrily. "Pick up that butter for me, Hugh, please." But she handed him her other packages and picked it up herself before he could make a move. The bag had split, the butter almost fell out again. Each block was neatly rectangular, right-angled at one end, at the other grubby, dented, out of shape. Her fingers tried to straighten these ends to shape – not looking, though, her eyes again were following her son, Penn.

"We're going in a minute," Anna called back.

"I just want to fetch something from indoors, that's all," said Jean.

"Be good tonight," Penn's mother said, and added as an afterthought, "Say goodnight to Penn for me, in case I don't see him. Oh and take that baby home, will you, take him home *soon*."

Hugh helped carry the things in from the car, then thankfully escaped. When he got back upstairs again, he went with reluctance into Jean's room, to find Anna alternately sulking and shaking with hysterical laughter, Jean curbing her, rather red in the face and cross, on the edge of tears herself, Hugh realized.

"And where have you been," she snapped at him, "leaving us to manage on our own. You didn't even say you were going out."

"I didn't know I had to."

"I suppose you haven't thought what we're going to do either?"

"No. Have you? It was all right this time anyway. She didn't recognize him."

"I almost wish she had," said Jean.

Hugh did not tell her what he had wished. But Anna, stopped laughing or sulking, came out of her own world into theirs again.

"Oh no," she said, "that would have spoiled it." And hugged Penn to her, frantically. "Anyway she wouldn't have dared," she said.

Even if the infant Penn had given them much chance it would have been impossible to settle to anything that evening. Once he slept all three of them retired into separate worlds of anxiety. Hugh roamed a great deal, from the top of the house to the bottom, and back again.

All evening he was afraid that his mother would question Penn's absence; was relieved that she did not, but annoyed on the other hand that she could be so vague, so careless as not to be more curious or worried as to his whereabouts. He wanted her to worry almost as much as he did not want her to.

She dropped a tray of dishes on the floor at one

point. He was rent by shock; he thought at first the worst had happened, the thing he waited for and feared, before he remembered that what he feared was the discovery of Penn, which would not be heralded in such a way. From the expressions on their faces both Jean and Anna must have suffered, briefly, the same fearful illusion.

All three of them helped pick the dishes up again, more or less willing; Anna also looked amused. By a miracle nothing was broken except for an already cracked plate, which had split in half neatly, along its crack.

"I wish you'd be more like other mothers sometimes," Jean said, her voice sharper than usual.

"Other people do occasionally drop things. Even you, Jean, I've known."

"But not all the time. You break something practically every day. Last week you broke my favourite bowl."

"Things taste the same out of other bowls."

"I think you enjoy it," said Jean bitterly, "breaking things."

"It's not what you do, *I* mind," said Hugh as bitterly, "it's what you don't do. What's funny then?" he snapped at Anna, seeing her little, separate smile.

"Nothing. *Nothing*," Anna said.

"Now leave that poor girl alone, Hugh."

"It's nothing to do with you." Hugh challenged his mother for a moment, before both of them looked away. Her "Don't speak to me like that," also came out somewhat lamely; this time neither of them seemed to want a fight. Hugh attacked his omelette instead. His mother ate hers absently, as if she couldn't taste what she was eating.

"Will Penn want something when he comes in? What time *will* he be in?" she asked not with much interest, but as if she thought she ought to inquire at least. Hugh's mumble satisfied her. "I gave him my key," he added, so that she would not be surprised that the doorbell did not ring; that is, if she wondered anything.

The kitten which had slept for most of the day came to life now. It went mad, leaping huge, stiff-legged leaps from side to side, dashing from one end of the room to the other, spinning furiously in pursuit of its shadow or its tail. It seemed to turn on its own axis, it seemed weightless like a shadow, or a feather – afterwards it tore round and round the room again, then paused, pounced, paused and pounced, time after time after time.

"All kittens behave like that," said Jean pro-prietorially. It helped distract them for a little while; till Hugh's father arrived and monopolized attention as always. He was much more interested in Anna, plying her with plums, a surprising number of which she ate. After a while she began to make patterns with the stones upon her plate, taking no notice of anyone, as if she was quite alone. Hugh tried to attract her attention once but she ignored him.

When Hugh went to bed he tossed and turned for hours; the landscape sucked him in eventually; he had resisted it, clinging to his bedhead even. But the bedhead was made of oak, which he did not know, because it was painted and he had never bothered to look any further. And the trees of course were oak trees too, in an avenue leading towards the castle. He had not yet reached the avenue. He was walking along a road towards it through a grey and familiar landscape, so familiar that though he only remembered being there four or five times, he must have visited it many other times that he did not remember.

The sun gave no brightness. It was as if its brilliant edges dwindled to a black centre. He stared at it fixedly for a minute, blinding himself, and so briefly afterwards saw nothing about him, except a kind of white, then grey, haze, from which emerged gradually the grey configurations of the landscape defuzzing slowly, growing darker, the outlines clear. The broken edges of the castle were like teeth.

Vision narrowed. It felt as if the landscape was an enormous eye, and he was at the centre of the eye. The immediate surroundings were grey, this centre black, and it was doing something to him that he fought against, against a force he could not define, until he realized it was trying to suck him in; that the blackness was both the pupil of the eye and a tunnel which was sucking, pulling him. Yet he was also still walking along a track; towards a castle. The actions co-existed, were carried on simultaneously. At the same time he was both screaming with fear and not screaming, feeling the harshness of the stones beneath his feet and not feeling them.

He struggled on. The castle grew nearer. The tunnel sucked as hard but did not manage to pull him farther in. The weight of the sky seemed to press on him too, pushing him into the tunnel,

into the pupil of the eye. It felt like being drowned
– only it would have to be a lake to drown him,
he thought confusedly, and not simply a tunnel.
At the same time these two opposing forces, raised
in him also a still greater obstinacy, a still greater
will to resist. He was actually walking faster and
then he was running, stumbling, and the forces
were having to pursue him. He had not burst out
of them exactly, as he had burst out of the circle
of alder trees in the first dream, they were still
there all round him, yet they did not stop him
going on. They were sensations as much as forces.
As he ran between the lines of oak trees – and they
were all dead he saw now – it was like a car passing
through an avenue of trees, with a little whoosh at
each tree, little stripes of sound all the way along,
except that these were stripes of feeling not of
sound; between each pair of trees he felt the pressures grow stronger.

He passed through a vast, an enormous pressure;
all the other pressures came with him and stopped
dead as he did, and then vaporized, faded from
him.

He had passed under the gate of the castle and
was inside it. He was in the courtyard, but the
castle was more or less a ruin.

He had escaped the eye, yet he was also at the
centre of it still, the eye being all around him. His
footsteps were loud on cracked cobblestones as he
walked towards a studded, oaken door. The studs
were multitudinous, and like eyes watching him,
they glinted with an iron glint, that seemed out of
place in this lightless, shineless world.

There was a handle on the door, shaped like a

bird; a crow. As he put his hand to it the world too faded. He found himself lying in darkness, in his own bed.

Hugh woke next morning from restless sleep to the sound of infant cheerfulness next door, and water running in the bathroom. Jean was down there rinsing nappies in the basin.

"Do you know what time he woke us, Hugh? Five o'clock, five *o'clock*. And we had to keep him quiet till now. We jolly well nearly came to wake you up to help."

Upstairs in Jean's room, Anna, who had slept in the little room next door looked disapproving. "Do you know he's wet right through to the mattress."

"Well what did you expect. Babies do, you know. It's not exactly as if we were practised at putting nappies on, and he wriggles such a lot."

Neither seemed as enthusiastic about baby-minding as they had been the day before. They were on the verge of quarrelling except when united against Hugh. Anna had never sided with Jean when Penn was here, Hugh thought.

Jean said, "We'll have to say that you and Penn had breakfast early and went out, Hugh."

"Does that mean I don't get any breakfast?"

"We'll bring you something. It will probably just have to be toast or something."

"I suppose that means I'll be left to look after him," said Hugh unenthusiastically, pointing at the baby who merely grinned back inanely. "He looks positively retarded this morning."

"It's about your turn. We've had him since yesterday. Look, you can feed him too. I've managed to bring up some cereal. But for goodness sake, Hugh, keep him quiet, *whatever*."

Jean did genuinely look tired. Her hair was like the fur on a not quite well cat, a little dull and spiky. She was wearing a brown-stoned brooch which she always wore like a mascot when she expected things to be difficult, Hugh noticed. Anna too was even paler than usual. He felt tired himself. He missed Penn, so, obviously, did Anna. But neither of them appeared as troubled as Jean.

Fortunately Jean remained maternal; it was she, not Anna, who checked the baby's nappy before she went downstairs, who set out Penn's food and made sure the room was safe. Anna merely stood and watched. Nor did she kiss the baby as Jean did, awkwardly, before they went out. But if she was less concerned about Penn, the baby, Hugh had the feeling she was more concerned about him as Penn, her elder brother; she turned back at the door, and for a longish moment gazed at him, before following Jean downstairs.

Hugh and Penn were left to stare each other out. Hugh had avoided such confrontations before. Now, uncomfortable, he was the first to look away. "Da," said the infant Penn, and held out the sodden looking cloth which up till then he'd been stuffing in his mouth. When Hugh did not respond, the baby seemed to realize that he did not know him, and also to notice that both the more familiar girls had gone. He started to crawl frantically towards the door. At the same time, his mouth squaring up, he let out an enormous howl.

Hugh, as frantically, grabbed him back. He tried

tickling Penn, bumped him up and down, made every face he could think of – the baby stopped wailing after a moment, but stared at him unblinking, unamused. He felt as foolish as an unsuccessful comic, was about to set him on the floor again when Penn jabbed a finger painfully right into his eye. It was Hugh who felt like howling now.

"Blast you, Penn," he said. And saying the name, had a sudden desperate vision: that this was Penn, his friend. He could not bear to think of that Penn now. Firmly he shut him from his mind, and remembered breakfast with relief; Weetabix and milk in a rabbit-covered bowl. Before Penn could start to wail again he thrust out a spoonful of the Weetabix – Penn obligingly opening his mouth, but shutting it again as the spoon arrived, so that it merely collided with his face and the Weetabix was scattered, mostly on the floor. The next time also, Penn opened his mouth to the approaching spoon only to push it aside with his fist, again effectively dispersing cereal, now largely over Hugh. Hugh fetched a towel, spread it on the floor and sat the baby in the middle of it. "You can jolly well feed yourself then," he said grimly and handed Penn the bowl and spoon. The next five minutes' peace was, he decided, worth the mess. Eating Weetabix with fingers was not exactly a tidy or a clean pursuit.

And after breakfast when Penn had first emptied out Jean's waste-paper basket and devoured a rotten apple-core, then attempted to annihilate Jean's collection of glass animals (not that that would have been much loss, Hugh thought privately) noisily resisting all attempts to interest him in the toys provided, Hugh reverted to the only proper distraction that he knew of: paint. There were two old tins of powder colour among his other materials. He mixed them, found sheets of newspaper and his oldest brushes, dabbing the newspaper with paint to encourage the baby and demonstrate the possibilities. The baby was much more interested in decorating itself than the paper, and by hand rather than by brush, but it freed Hugh for another five minutes, more or less, until Anna and Jean arrived back from breakfast with some leathery slices of toast for him.

Jean gasped, seeing the room.

"You didn't have to let him make such an awful mess. It's *awful*, Hugh."

"You must be joking," Hugh said wearily. "If I ever have babies I'm going to keep them in cages till they're old enough to be civilized. He practically gouged my eye out. Look."

"Just look at his cereal. It's everywhere. And paint, Hugh, paint for a baby of his age. You must be out of your mind."

"I suppose you would rather that he'd howled the place down," said Hugh and saw Anna smile secretly, "or broken all your glass animals. They're hideous anyway."

"Hugh, you've got to do something. We can't go on like this." Jean was scarlet in the face.

"Something like what?"

"Like . . . don't be so negative, Hugh."

"Well have you any ideas then?"

"I can't," she wailed, "I can't."

"Well nor have I. Unless we all get in the cupboard ourselves. That'll be the end of it. We'll be babies too, no one will be able to make us do anything."

"No," said Jean. "*No.*" Hugh could feel her terror, that she could scarcely speak for it, letting it run away with her.

"We could go and see that old man of yours," Anna said quietly to Hugh.

"What old man?" he feigned incomprehension. "Oh *him*. Just what good do you think he'd do?" He thought to himself, that's truer than you know; for nothing at all had come out of his going yesterday. The old man had been very unhelpful, and was just as likely to be unhelpful today; the situation being still the same. Positively he did not want to go back to him again. He was sick of the whole business suddenly. He wanted to go away, to shut everything out and paint. ALONE, he thought; by MYSELF. The thought was as loud to him as a spoken voice, it commanded him; so that he even turned to go out of the room, all the reasons why he should stay wiped clean out of his mind.

"Where are you going? You *can't* go away," Jean shouted after him.

"All right, let's put him in the cupboard again," Hugh said pointing at Penn, who was sitting in the centre of the room regarding them. The thought only came to his mind as he spoke.

"Are you serious?"

"Of course I am" (which was mostly, though, a lie).

"It *is* an idea," said Anna thoughtfully. Hugh looked at her with almost as much surprise as Jean did.

"But I don't see . . ."

"We've never tried putting anything back in there, have we? Something we've already changed." Nor had they; which struck Hugh now as odd, almost odd enough not to be an accident. "Suppose it worked the other way," went on Anna, persuasively.

"Just supposing it *didn't?*" Jean asked. She sounded calmer now. Even so her interruptions were irrelevant, more or less, Hugh and Anna discussing this as just between themselves.

"He'd only be younger . . ." said Hugh. "We wouldn't be worse off, would we?"

"It might be better," Anna said.

"It's all crazy, it couldn't be worse," Jean pushed her voice in forcibly.

"We could experiment with something else first, couldn't we," said Anna.

The infant Penn had started to crawl towards the door. They all suddenly saw and stopped and watched him.

"He *wants* to go himself," said Anna, drawing in her breath. They watched him pull the door open and disappear round it. They heard the door of Hugh's room pulled open in its turn – at which they all three looked at one another and followed. "Well, at least we won't need to clean him up," said Hugh. Penn went straight for the cupboard. Jean gasped and ran to pull him out, but it was tidier, the more obvious course, to let go, to shut the door on him. Hugh automatically, without any conscious decision-taking, removed Jean, and Anna, gently, carefully this time, closed the cupboard door. It felt as if another, inevitable piece had been fitted into a pattern, in which they and everything they knew now formed a part. Then – it was half-past nine on an August Friday – they opened the door again, to find what looked like an almost new-born baby lying there blinking up at them.

Their first thought was uniform, even Jean's; not shock or fear or horror – Hugh, without looking at them, knew neither of the others felt any of those, any more than he did himself. What he felt – and they felt – was a huge and quite simple awe.

The baby was so tiny, so puny and shrivelled. It could not have been more than a few days' old. But its face looked as old as an old man's face, the skin all dried and wrinkled round its eyes and ears. Its legs kicked thin as a sparrow's legs from the fat white folds of its napkin. When Jean laid it gently down on Hugh's bed it lay with its eyes wide open, dark yet milky, staring up at the ceiling, and there was a piece of fluff in the centre of one eye. The baby did not seem to mind the fluff. He watched its mouth opening and shutting, its arms and legs moving randomly, slowly. It was there in the room with the rest of them and yet somehow far away, kicking and hitting at something none of them could see.

CHAPTER FOURTEEN

Jean and Anna took turns at carrying the baby down the hill. Penn was much too small to go in the pushchair now, and there was no possibility of getting hold of a pram instead. They had found a shawl in the tallboy from which both the button box and the napkins had come – it must have been white once, but was now faintly yellow and smelt of mothballs. It reminded Hugh of occasions quite other than these, little flashes of himself as a child playing with something or dreaming or watching his mother turn out those same drawers, digging in them frenetically like a terrier, in order to find some garment or piece of material.

The baby, well-wrapped in first the shawl and then a check tablecloth to disguise its existence as far as possible, was asleep; well-fed, replete. Despite the circumstances both Jean and Anna looked pleased with themselves, as well they might, thought Hugh, having observed with surprise the somewhat technical operations necessary for feeding it.

The baby had begun whimpering not long after it came out of the cupboard. "It must be hungry," Jean and Anna had said more or less simultaneously, and both had turned and looked at Hugh.

"Why are you looking at me? I don't know the first thing about feeding babies."

But neither Anna or Jean, it appeared, knew much about feeding either. They seemed scared by

Penn's smallness, holding him gingerly as if he was about to break. They could have given Penn a bottle, but did not know how to prepare it, and had to scour the house for discarded baby manuals which would instruct them. Everything had to be sterilized by boiling, it appeared, including the water to make up the feed, and there had to be the right proportion of milk and the right proportion of water, and to assess that they had to know the baby's weight. All of this meant expeditions to the kitchen, first to weigh Penn on Hugh's mother's old-fashioned scales – half the brass weights were missing which did not help – then to boil pans of water, Hugh keeping guard meanwhile in case his mother came. The baby continued wailing on and off, a small noise like a kitten, but very persistent. It made little sucking, snuffling sounds, trying unavailingly to eat its thumb as a substitute for food.

To distract himself, Hugh read out loud extracts from the baby manual. "The one thing a mother needs to know; what is best for baby's needs, and what sort of balance to aim for; breast or bottle, let mother choose herself, and what suits her is bound to be good for baby." He so annoyed the already agitated Jean and Anna that they told him, in unison, *they* weren't going to buy the tin of milk from the supermarket, the teat from the chemist; *he* was. Luckily for him, they said, he did not have to buy a bottle too, as Jean had unearthed one from the back of the airing-cupboard.

There was a queue in the chemist's this time, though still only one assistant. As he waited he heard a familiar voice behind him.

"Hugh," it said. He turned to find of all people the one he least wanted to see, apart from his own mother, that is; Penn's mother. Her dark eyes were ringed with black this morning – paint maybe, or exhaustion, after her night out – for once she reminded him less of a bird than of some nocturnal mammal; a bushbaby for example, like the one he'd seen at the zoo. How extraordinary to think he'd been at the zoo, looking at bushbabies, only two days ago. It felt more like a hundred years. The colour running to his face, he attempted to be as nonchalant as Anna had been the day before.

"Did you have a good evening?" he asked politely. He was doing quite well listening to her telling him at length why it hadn't been good, it had been terrible, when he noticed, to his horror, that the queue ahead of him had dwindled, and the last person in it, an old woman in a bulbous green hat, was handing over the money for a box of corn-plasters and a tin of blackcurrant lozenges. Any moment it would be his turn.

But he could not ask for the teat in front of Penn's mother. Suppose she told *his* mother about it, too? What would they think? He tried desperately to imagine some other use for a teat for a baby's bottle which might explain his buying one; unable to imagine any use at all, he mumbled something and almost ran across the shop to a display of extravagantly wrapped and ribboned soaps, at which he stared as if absorbed, actually seeing none of them.

"You'll pay half as much again for the wrapping if you buy those," said the voice of Penn's mother behind him. "If you want it for a present, why

don't you buy some separately and wrap it yourself, a creative gent like you."

Hugh continued to stare fixedly at three green
heart-shaped cakes in a heart-shaped box, labelled
"Amour – Springtime."

"Can I *help* you," came another voice, for the
third time of asking, he realized; only he had been
too agitated to notice.

"Help her," he said, somewhat desperately,
pointing at Penn's mother. "I'm not in any hurry."

"No, no, Hugh, I'm not in a hurry either. Get
what you want," she said solicitously, grinning at
him in such a way, however, he wondered if she
was teasing him; knowing Penn's mother, most
likely.

"*Take* your time then, *sir*," said the assistant, as
pert as ever in her pink overall. Hugh, seeing no
help for it, snatched from the rack before him the
cheapest soap he could see, shaped like a lemon
and wrapped in tissue paper.

"That's twenty pence to you, *sir*," she said.
Reluctantly, hoping he'd still have enough left for
the milk and the teat, he counted out the money.
Anna and Jean must be wondering where he'd got
to. But there was nothing he could do about that.

"Hope they took that baby back," Penn's
mother threw at him then, making his stomach
turn. "I don't mind those two walking other people's dogs. But *babies*." But she turned to ask for
a packet of Elastoplast as he gathered up his soap,
he was able to escape without answering. He went
next door to the newsagents and stood gazing at
boxes of felt-tipped pens and black rubber insects.
He had been afraid that Penn's mother might

follow him in there, too, but to his relief saw her leave the chemist's, climb into her white Renault standing outside, and drive off smartly, as neat and direct a performance as any of Penn's on some sport's field – this could not be said of the way Hugh's own mother drove. She waved as she went. Hugh was not sure whether the wave was meant for him or for some other acquaintance she had caught sight of along the street.

He went back to the chemist's shop. It was empty now, to his relief.

"Large, medium or small?" asked the assistant, standing on a stool to get the teat from the shelf above the counter. She had her blond hair in a ponytail, he noticed.

"Large . . . *what*?" asked the baffled Hugh, removing his gaze to her (thick, he observed) ankles. "Hole, of course. In the teat. Large, medium or small. Wake up, dozy, make up your mind," she urged as Hugh hesitated. "I can't stand here all day, anyone would think you liked looking at my legs." And she giggled, again; making Hugh think of Anna. She annoyed him as much as Anna. Anna liked annoying him, too.

He considered the smallness of the baby. "Small, I suppose," he said at last.

"Got an addition to the family, then?" asked the assistant, putting the teat in a paper bag, her voice marginally more friendly. "Not exactly," Hugh said, blushing again. He'd been about to add something lame about a friend's baby, when he decided it was nothing to do with her. Why shouldn't he buy a teat if he wanted, why should he have to explain? He handed over the money and emerged from the shop almost dizzy with relief, so dizzy indeed that he forgot the tin of milk till he was almost halfway home, and had to go back to the supermarket, where he found himself waiting at the checkout behind a woman buying a dozen tins of pilchards; for her children, it appeared, not cats. (If it had been her cats, she explained to Hugh, she would have bought the kind without tomato sauce.)

All he had left afterwards was one half pence. Penn's going to have to pay me back, he thought, when all this is over. Yes. *Over*, he thought. He could not bear to imagine it would not all sort itself out in the end; how, though, he could not imagine. Any more than he could imagine what they were to do if they needed to buy anything else. But it was Penn they'd spent all the money on; so when things were sorted out, Penn would have to pay them back. Of course he could have the lemon soap if he wanted, Hugh thought. He certainly did not.

They fed the baby in Penn's room, the one corresponding to Hugh's in the next-door house. Anna said it would be safer, her mother wasn't expected back till the afternoon. In Hugh's house, their mother might turn up at any minute.

He shouldn't have bought the teat with the small hole, it turned out; the smaller the baby, Jean said, the larger the hole had to be, because small babies sucked so much less powerfully. This one couldn't get any milk at all through the small-holed teat; after sucking away valiantly for a minute or two, it began to howl. "How was I supposed to know what size to get?" said Hugh, disgustedly – all the same it was his idea that they enlarged the hole by heating a needle, and pushing that through. Next time the baby tried to suck it succeeded, judging by the contented gulps and the way the level of milk in the bottle began going down.

They took it in turns to give the bottle. Hugh did not think it was anything he wanted to do at first. But after he had watched both Anna and Jean first clutch the baby awkwardly till they grew used to it, then soften, become easier, when he saw how still they sat, how intently they gazed, smiling a little into the baby's face, a great longing came over him to feed the baby too. At last he could bear it no longer, Jean's turn in his view had lasted long enough; he took the baby firmly from her, sat down on Penn's bed, baby in one hand, bottle in the other.

Its papery looking finger nails were surprisingly long and sharp. The clutch of its small fingers, the pull of its suck against the bottle made him feel strange; he felt the same awe as on first seeing the baby. At the same time he felt an unfamiliar soft- ness and warmth. He must look as rapt, as intent, he thought, as Jean and Anna had. Neither of them objected to his feeding the baby. Indeed neither seemed surprised, though Jean looked worried at first, and afterwards teased him a little, fiddling as she did so with her brown-stoned brooch. Anna said nothing. She did not take her eyes off either of them, Hugh or the baby.

The small warmth of the baby against him becoming the more comfortable as time went on, his eyes began to wander round the room. He began to notice all over again the evidence of

Penn's sporting activities; a cricket bat, two tennis rackets, a squash racket, arranged in meticulous order; Penn was – had been – meticulously neat. On a shelf above there were books on sport, books on the sea by Masefield and Conrad, a whole series of novels by Alexander Kent, and a big old-fashioned edition of King Arthur and his Knights. Next to the books was a silver cup won for school athletics, pinned above the bed a row of photographs, of sportsmen mostly, footballers and cricketers, but also one of Jane Fonda, dressed in leather; all the familiar paraphenalia of Penn's ordinary life.

It made Hugh miss wretchedly the real Penn. It made him ache. At the same time he saw all these things as he never had seen them before. Staring down at the baby's clutching fingers, he could not imagine them big enough to hold the cricket bat or the rackets – compared to the baby these looked not only huge, they looked grotesque. He thought of Gulliver in Brobdingnag. From the baby's eye view the graining of willow on the cricket bat, of oak on the bookshelves, was crude not to say coarse; the gut strings of the racket appeared swollen; disgusting, he thought. The books, too, were books for giants.

When Anna removed the baby from him, a moment later, firmly, saying "It's my turn now," he did not protest. He went to Penn's bookshelves and took down the big volume of King Arthur and his Knights. He opened it at the end; to find a picture of an island covered in blossoming apple trees, of knights lying among them accompanied by beautiful maidens. In the distance was a castle; on the page opposite the word; Avalon. Paradise,

it said; the place to which Arthur came and his
knights, where they found immortality, so lived
for ever in a golden world. Thomas the Rhymer
might have left fairyland and the fairy queen and
come back to the earth, but these knights did not
leave Avalon; they would never have to face the
kind of problems he was facing, Hugh thought
enviously. How good, he thought, gazing at them
hungrily, how much better to stay with the apple
trees; apple trees of immortality, of course, that's
what the old man meant. Better to stay with the
fairy queen, too, assuming she was part of Avalon;
he thought she must be. Fairyland. Paradise.
Avalon. They were all one and the same. But then
he turned back to look at the room; at the baby;
at his sister Jean and her friend, Anna, both gazing
down at the baby with an expression on their faces
he had never seen there before, and in a moment
of unaccustomed warmth and affection, he was not
so sure.

The baby took a long time to feed. At half-past
eleven Jean said, with a gasp, "Look at the time.
We'll have to hurry or we won't have time before
lunch." She and Anna decided to abandon the last
ounce. The baby was almost asleep now, and kept
on forgetting to suck.

It was Hugh's idea that they should go back to
the junk shop and certainly not his wish. But he
had to admit he had no better ideas about what
they should do. Nor, unwilling to confess his visit
yesterday, quite why he did not know, could he
justify his insistence it was likely to be a waste of
time.

While organizing the feed, the simple pressure

of activity had driven away their fear and apprehension. But walking down the hill it all came back. No one spoke. Every person they met might have been about to ask what they were doing with so small a baby, might threaten to take it away. The traffic had never seemed noisier, grinding past them, up and down the slope. As for the ordinary, familiar trees – Hugh looked at them as if for the first time in his life and thought – realized – that they were nothing more nor less than giant plants, and as such not ordinary or familiar at all; on the contrary. He might have been Gulliver again in the kingdom of the giants – not a comfortable feeling; not comfortable at all.

The shop was shut, and looked empty. The windows were so dusty it was hard to see anything beyond, even on the window itself. By pressing his face to the glass and screwing up his eyes Hugh could make out a few dim shapes, but that was all. The screen of dust might have been formed deliberately to hide them from the outside world. Other people must have come to the conclusion that the shop was empty too, because two posters with flowing lettering to advertise a pop group called Stoned Crow had been posed in one corner of the window. CLOSED, said the notice on the door.

Having got so far, in spite of his reluctance to come, Hugh did not intend to go away without seeing the old man. He took the door handle and rattled it furiously, at the same time knocking at the glass with his other hand. Jean and Anna stood a few paces behind him, Anna holding the baby.

"But if he's *shut*," Jean was saying despairingly.

On the other side of the door, within the shop, Hugh thought he discerned faint movements. Rage overcame him, he was determined to get an answer, rattling and knocking harder than ever. "You'll break the door down," Jean said anxiously. But the door had suddenly removed itself from his hands and stood wide open.

The old man blinked in the daylight, his voice came slight and querulous. "What do you want? Can't you see I'm closed."

Hugh said fiercely: "You've got to let us in."

"Got to. *Got* to. I don't understand that."

"You know perfectly well who I am. You must help us, you must." The old man looked at him with what appeared to be dislike. "Must, *must*. Must, is it?" He stared at each of them in turn. Hugh and Anna both stared back unblinkingly, but Jean, uneasily, turned away her head. He did not look at the baby in Anna's arms, just touched it briefly with an expression across his face that Hugh could not read. The baby stirred but did not wake.

"Come in. If you *must*," the old man said at last.

"We must," Hugh said, and stepped across the threshold. The two girls followed him.

"You chose the cupboard yourself. You did not buy it because I persuaded you."

Hugh did not reply. He was looking round the shop. As he had guessed when peering from outside it was even emptier than yesterday. There were still the objects – all with that same face – but fewer; there was still the same sense of recognition, yet if anything he could trace it even less than yesterday. The old man had disappeared again, and they stood in the middle of the shop waiting for his return. Hugh found himself overcome with unexpected embarrassment, wishing himself anywhere else but here. He shrank from the thought of having to explain himself again, of having to ask questions. He wished he could shut his eyes and vanish.

The old man returned to the shop very differently. He was almost jovial. "Now what can I do to help?" he asked as if they were favoured customers. They stared at him in surprise, but no one said anything. Jean looked anxiously at Hugh, but Hugh ignored the message. Anna had begun wandering round the shop, picking things up and putting them down again; peering at pictures on the walls; wiping off dust with her fingers where she wanted to examine more closely. She had given the baby to Jean to hold.

"Now then, you must have come for something. You'd better tell me quickly or I shall have to send you away again." But he said it as if he was joking.

"You know," said Hugh, "you know perfectly well. The cupboard," he added reluctantly, the old man looking at him, still with a smile, but without a word. "You've got to help. Look, that's Penn, that baby, he should be the same age as me. But look what it's done to him."

"What did you expect? I don't see why you're complaining. It's a fine child."

"I told you." Hugh, goaded, was getting angrier. "Just a cupboard to put my clothes in. And just look now." He pointed at Penn.

"Well and what ideas have you?"

"None," admitted Hugh.

"He did have one. He said we should all get into

the cupboard ourselves. But what good would that do?" asked Jean, rather loud and shrill at first, reducing the volume halfway through, because of the baby sleeping in her arms.

The old man spoke to Hugh. "You have already been inside it."

Hugh stared at him. "What do you mean?"

"Use your head," said the old man mildly.

"I wanted to be inside it. I nearly got into it. But I didn't, otherwise what happened to Penn would have happened to me."

"What happened to Penn frightened you a good deal more than it frightened him."

"He's just a baby now. He wouldn't understand anything."

"*You* were frightened."

"I don't know." Hugh spoke with less certainty. But as he spoke a coldness came over him; at first a wave of cold, and then, more swiftly, of heat – panic – which swept through every part of him; he was trembling with fear. He had to sit down for a minute. But there was nothing to sit on except a cane chest, which seemed so fragile under him that he rose almost at once, only to reseat himself, with infinite care this time, as if to show he was not so carried away by terror that he could not recognize the need for care. Yet he had been carried away by terror. Sulkily, unwillingly, he admitted it at last.

"OK," he said. "I was scared. I was scared some of the time."

"Where there is no fear there is no decision. It's because you are afraid that you have to decide, not him." The old man looked fleetingly, for the first time, at the baby in Jean's arms.

"You said all that before. It doesn't help."

"Then I will help you a little. Let me point out, for instance, that the cupboard is more powerful than you think. In a sense it has drawn you inside itself already."

"What do you mean? *I* haven't been inside the cupboard," he said, afraid all over again.

"I don't understand either," said Jean, her voice rising, as if to defend Hugh. The old man ignored her.

"Use your head, boy," he urged again.

"Those – dreams – I had . . ." began Hugh, reluctantly.

"Dreams. Dreams." The old man's voice was infinitely scornful now. "Call them that if you want. If you can only accept definitions, categories, you know already. Dreams!"

"There's nothing wrong with dreams," said Hugh.

"Who said there was? Don't be so touchy, boy."

"*Me*, touchy?" Yet the matter was suddenly engrossing Hugh.

He asked, slowly. "Was it really some other world. Like Thomas the Rhymer's fairyland? – like Avalon; something like that? But it wasn't any more real than a dream; or any less come to that. Just different," he admitted.

"Why shouldn't it be different and still real?" said the old man.

"I never said it shouldn't be different, I never said it wasn't real," said Hugh. As he spoke he noticed Jean staring at him, her eyes wide.

"What was wrong with being frightened?" asked the old man.

Hugh said crossly, "You keep changing the subject. You keep on asking me the same questions, and not answering any. We keep on going round and round in circles."

"Was it so bad?" insisted the old man.

"I wasn't frightened then."

"But you were just now?"

"That was just for Penn," Hugh said.

"Because he did not come out?"

"If I went in, I came out the same. How could I if he didn't? Anyway what happened to me is beside the point. It's *him*, Penn, we're here about."

"All right, you were frightened. But is that important? If so I suppose, naturally, you want to do something."

"You talk as if this was an ordinary thing to happen. It's reasonable enough to want some way out – of a thing like this – " Hugh indicated Penn again. "Of *course* I want an answer."

"You could call it an answer. The name is unimportant."

"In which case I'll call what happened to me dreams. Why can't you talk sense?" said Hugh, furiously.

("What's in a name," Anna quoted dreamily in what he would have called a very prissy voice, the first time she had spoken since they left the house.) Hugh was angry in part because totally confused. It was like a conversation in a dream in which no comment related or led on to any other.

"We want Penn back at his own proper age," he said speaking loudly and clearly, as if to an idiot or a foreigner. "I'm asking you for advice not for philosophy." He was offensive intentionally.

"But you already know. You don't need advice. You're only resisting it. You have been into that other world. Now go into it again, but deliberately. And go on into your castle."

Hugh drew in his breath. "There really is a castle?" he asked slowly.

"Don't you believe it yet?"

"I didn't mean it quite like that."

On a table nearby a chessboard was set out. The kings, both black and white, had faces, the same face of course as all the others. And there were castles – the obviousness of this annoyed Hugh as his gaze fell on them. Yet he still could not stop himself reaching out and picking up one black and one white castle, one in either hand, balancing, turning them, setting them down again. The black castle was slightly the heavier of the two. An ebony castle, he thought, and an ivory castle; a castle of wood and another of bone. "Corny," he said aloud, still irritated. "Corny. I bet you put them there on purpose. They weren't here yesterday."

The old man picked up the white castle now and stroked and held it cupped between his hands. "In the castle you can try to decide. You will see what the choices are, as they are, not as you see them now."

Hugh was observing the way the castle trembled in his hands. They were knotted, with huge blue veins, very old, very shrivelled hands. He was such an *old* man, he realized, and felt an inconvenient, disconcerting sympathy and pity; which made him feel guilty at his own impatience. Age made you ramble as the old man had seemed to ramble. And yet always within his words there had been this uncompromising edge.

The sleeping baby in Jean's arms pursed up its lips with its usual sucking sound. Hugh looked from him to the old man and back again, drawing in his breath at the likeness between them; the way both appeared withered, flesh narrow over bone. Almost for the first time he could see a progression between birth and youth and age; not as unlinked stages – like snapshots, or separate beads on a string – baby, child, youth, young man, middle-aged then old, man – but as one steady progression from each stage to the next. That would be his own progression. He had never related it to himself before, or only vaguely, not with this total, piercing comprehension. Growing old was the worst of it. One day he would be pitied as he pitied this old man. How could you bear it, he wondered.

"Do I wait . . ." he began angrily, but the inconvenient pity for the old man overtaking his fear and rage, he repeated much more gently, "Do I have to wait till I dream again?"

"It is *not* a dream."

"So you keep saying." Hugh was angry again. "But what else do I call it?"

"Go into the cupboard. Don't wait for it to pull you, enter of your own will. Then your power will be greater and its the less."

"By myself?" asked Hugh.

"Don't be more stupid than are. All four of you. Of course."

"Do I have to go?" Jean looked more terrified than ever. "I couldn't go."

"Especially you. It has less power over you."

"Oh *please*," Jean said. "Oh *please*, oh *please*."

"Must *I* go?" asked Anna.

"Is it dangerous?" asked Hugh.

"You wear me out with questions," he answered querulously, almost whining. When asked outright for pity, Hugh stopped feeling it. "You'd better tell us, you must," he said, growing angry again.

"*Must*? Of course it's dangerous; use your wits. Making choices always is."

"Choices? What choices?" asked Hugh.

"Those have to be chosen too," said the old man.

"We only want Penn back at his proper age, that's all we want." Jean was crying now, tears pouring down her cheeks. She had to give the baby to Anna to hold, so that she could hunt for a handkerchief.

"Do you? How easy you make it sound."

"Is that all you have to say?" asked Hugh. The old man indicated his weeping sister. "Maybe it is easier for her than it is for you or for her" – here he indicated Anna; or maybe he was indicating Penn. "That's all I can say. Isn't it enough?"

The old man's voice was more querulous than ever. He sounded very tired. There was a silence in which all three of them looked at each other and away again, and from which the old man, who had for a moment seemed to forget their existence, suddenly swung round on Anna and the baby and let loose at them a flood of words, his voice stronger than it had been all morning. They listened to him bewildered and amazed.

"Of course I look ordinary. What do you expect?

All of us were ordinary in most respects. Everything is ordinary, how would it be tolerable otherwise? – dying, loving, being born, it's all dirty sheets and bowls of water, it's where to find breakfast and where supper, eating and drinking and pissing and weeping. No matter how long you live for, it always is like that and it always was; except sometimes, occasionally, in a moment. Just for a moment. And I've not much time left for that, and what time there is you're wasting."

They watched him, mute; Hugh was almost holding his breath. The old man's voice had wandered towards the end. Now it hardened again.

"Go away all of you. You're wearing me out. I need what strength I have and I need what time. What you do now is up to you; you have the one chance that's all, just as I had, you can use the thing as you like. Go away and do it. Go away."

Hugh looked back as they filed out. For a brief moment before the door was slammed on them and the bolts noisily drawn, he saw the old man's face, very pale and as if hanging in mid air, his body lost in the gloom, and beyond him all the other faces, carved or painted or engraved, from the chess kings of ebony and ivory to the brown-spotted prints on the walls. The blind white head was in a corner. He had not noticed it this morning, not till now, but it too, he realized, bore the same features as the rest.

"What was it all about? All that last bit?" he asked Anna as they started up the hill. They had dropped behind Jean, who was no longer crying but walking silently and very stiffly for her, and whispered to each other, almost as if they preferred her not to hear. (In Hugh's case he might have been afraid of frightening her still more than she was frightened already; even though the old man had hinted that she had less reason to be frightened than anyone else.) "He seemed to be talking to you, Anna," he said, "Particularly."

"Didn't you see all those faces?" Anna asked. Hugh knew what she was going to say next; had known it all the time; had not wanted to know. "They were all the same face. They were all of him only younger, some younger than others."

Hugh sighed. He tested Anna. "But they all came from different times. There was a Roman head and an eighteenth century print and a mediaeval . . ."

"He had the cupboard; that's the point," said Anna. "Perhaps it wasn't a cupboard always. Perhaps he made it into a cupboard, or someone did."

"But then why . . . ?" pressed Hugh. Anna interrupted him. "I was thinking how ordinary he looked if it worked like that; if he'd been alive so long. He must have picked up my thought." She smiled tentatively at Hugh. Hugh, lightly, touched her on the arm. And a moment later touched her arm again. "Now it's up to us. Now it's our turn," he said.

CHAPTER FIFTEEN

Hugh's mother called out from the kitchen as they went quietly up the stairs. "Hugh, Jean, food's nearly ready." "Five minutes, *five*," Hugh shouted back.

They shut the door of his room and wedged it with a chair. As usual they had to wait for Anna who insisted on combing her hair very carefully. But at last, still without saying anything, they climbed into the cupboard, first Anna, holding the baby – she had taken it from Jean without a word, just holding out her arms, Jean surrendering without protest – then Jean, then last, Hugh himself. He had intended to leave the door open, but involuntarily gave a tug on the tie-rail and the door clicked into place behind him. "Don't shut the other one, *don't*," Jean pleaded. Hugh had no intention of it, yet the door swung shut, seemingly of its own accord, set off by the movement of the other one. He put out his hand to stop it, too late, for the latch caught, and when he tried pushing it open, it appeared to have jammed. He could not open either door.

Jean was sobbing quietly beneath her breath. She was trying to disguise it, but every now and then a louder one broke out as a hiccup and a gasp. Hugh felt for her hand in the darkness and took it and squeezed it, and she squeezed back gratefully. He wanted to take Anna's hand too, tentatively put out his own, but as he hesitated heard a whimper and remembered that she was holding the baby.

The baby whimpered again. The whole cupboard smelt of baby, the faintly sweet animal smell of milk, wet nappy and talcum powder. It was a big cupboard – yet Hugh would have expected it to feel much more crowded than it did, with the three of them and Penn inside it. But it felt as if the darkness reached for miles behind him, as if the back of the cupboard was not there at all, and when he reached out his spare hand it was almost a shock to find the cool grain of the wood beneath his fingers.

The grain, the whole feel of the wood was good, comforting. Hugh traced it out, his fingers almost as seeing as eyes, and he took Jean's hand, the one he held, and placed it on the wood, so that she could feel it and be comforted as well.

He did not remember ever holding Jean's hand before. As a family they did not often hug or kiss or touch. Penn and Anna's family was much more demonstrative.

There was a sound in the cupboard now, a single note, yet containing all notes. At first it emerged from a single point, but then it hissed and swelled, spread further as if beyond the walls, as if thrown out into an enormous void. But at the same time it seemed to have joined itself into a narrower line of sound, like a telegraph wire above Hugh's head, and he reached up his hand to find the brass hanging-rail which felt as thin and hard as he expected, but also alive, as if full of electricity, making his wrists, his arms, his hands tingle and shake with sound, with the echoings it threw so far away. The echoes seemed held and thrown by other places too. Hugh felt them by his hips but thinner, from the tie-rail that must have been, also by his head in triplicate, a more florid, curling sound, no doubt emerging from the three brass hooks. The sound ran down his arms, up into his head, until it seemed filled with the same echoes, filled with humming, heated wires, hissing, swelling, exploding. It was unbearable. Hugh cried out sharply, dropped Jean's hand and clutched at his head with both hands. The echoes died. The darkness faded. It was like being in some vehicle, rushing towards a group of trees, the vision glassy and shimmering with the speed of it – he put out his hands to protect his head from collision, but then the world steadied about him. He was standing on the edge of a wood, dizzy still but no longer moving, quiet, in one place.

"That was a real bramble, it really hurt," said an indignant voice. He looked round to see Jean holding out her leg, with a line of red beads in one place, on a white graze.

"And that's real blood, so it can't be a dream, Hugh."

"Who said it was a dream?" Jean looked at him and nodded. She seemed much calmer. She was no longer crying, nor looked as if she wanted to. They stood side by side looking about them. The wood at their backs was low and scrubby, with untidy undergrowth, brambles and nettles and stunted saplings, and underfoot dead twigs and branches and the bleached-out leaves of many autumns; soft beneath but still faintly crisp on top.

"Look, apples," Jean said, and Hugh's eyes following hers saw a young apple tree. It had only four apples on it, much too round and weighty for the slender tree – "They're ripe," Jean said, "do you think we dare eat one?" Hugh was tempted too. As Jean was not tall enough he himself reached up and picked the nearest green though ripe-looking apple, but an instinctive caution stopped him taking a bite out of it. "I'm not sure, I'm not sure it would be safe. Perhaps we'd better not." Jean, cautious herself, accepted his caution without argument. Hugh put the apple in the pocket of his jeans where it made an awkward bulge and rubbed against his thigh as he moved. It was the first time in this place he had not been wearing pyjamas, he realized. How absurd he must have looked here in striped pyjamas from Marks and Spencers. Though this thought had never occurred to him at the time, he did, undoubtedly, feel easier in his jeans and T-shirt. He felt part of the country, belonging to it, instead of standing out as an intruder, a stranger, even though on the face of it, jeans, T-shirts, were no more appropriate.

The familiar landscape reached away. Part of its very familiarity, he thought, lay precisely in the way it changed each time he came, not just seasonally but in its very features. What was absent to his eyes was still held in his mind, was part of what he saw – just as some aspects of a friend may not be visible yet still remain part of him. And that he knew was a good analogy; this landscape assuming personality, assuming life as landscape in his own familiar world did not. There was no lake today for instance, but he recognized other landmarks – folds and dips and rises, groups and avenues of trees. The castle dominated everything. It was whole, no longer ruined, no longer forbidding, wrapped in sunlight, slumbering, peaceful. Yet it was also the centre of a vortex, drawing everything in towards it on invisible threads. It was like the twist of a kaleidoscope. The same elements formed a different pattern, but the pattern had always been present in the elements, the castle assumed only its obvious, rightful place.

"Is that where we're going? Is that your castle?"

"I guess so; I can't see another one."

"You've been here before. How many times?"

"Every night since the cupboard came. That I remember anyway." Jean drew in her breath. "Have you been into the castle?" "Only once, that I remember. And not right inside, just into a court-yard. It was ruined then." Hugh wished he had not added this. Jean's voice became higher, more anxious. "But how could it be? It isn't ruined now."

"It was probably just the way I saw it," he said to comfort her.

Jean said wonderingly: "I didn't know it would be like *this*."

"Like how?"

"Ordinary."

"*Ordinary?*" asked Hugh.

"Grass and trees and brambles which prick you. It's like the park. I mean, like any walk." "What did you think it would be like?" "I don't know, I didn't know – I couldn't – but not like this. Like any bit of country. And it's such a fantastic day."

It was too, the best day of any that Hugh had been here, high summer, with a gentle easy sun, the heat not at all oppressive. The air hummed with insect notes, with the sudden chirpings of strong-legged grasshoppers, which stopped as abruptly as they started; high above there was a solitary lark. After the confusion of the cupboard everything seemed as simple, as clear-cut as its song. "I wonder where Penn and Anna are?" Jean asked, but she did not seem alarmed by the lack of an answer. The castle neither welcomed nor threatened them, and they walked towards it between swathes of green bracken, sharp-smelling and full of insect life. Beyond was grass burned pale yellow; it looked silky at a distance but felt prickly and brittle to walk through and to touch.

The path here was so narrow it could only have been made by rabbits. Jean went on ahead of Hugh. But suddenly, as they came round a curve of bracken which had temporarily blocked their view, she stopped dead, gasped and clung to him, her calm not as secure as it had seemed. "Look, *look*," she said.

A little way ahead of them, picking its way across the rough ground, with swaying, jogging quarters, was the horse that Hugh had seen before, and on it the same rider. "It's Penn," Jean said, and the rider turning Hugh saw that she was right. The red hair was unmistakable. It looked as if he had seen them too because he jerked with his arm, up and forward, then spurred on the horse which moved into a canter, then a gallop. Jean dropped Hugh's arm, stood for a moment, irresolute, touching her brown-stoned brooch. Then she started to run after him, stumbling, once almost falling. She stopped, seeing how hopeless it was, and waited for Hugh to catch up.

"It looks as if he's going to the castle too," she said. And then, with a start, "He isn't a baby any more."

"No. He's a man," Hugh said.

They were walking on a paved track now which led straight down towards the castle. There had been an avenue of oak trees along it yesterday and even without them a shadow seemed to fall across Hugh's mind. "Look at the orchards," Jean said; "I've never seen so many apple trees."

Nor indeed had Hugh. Before it had seemed as if the castle had stood on the edges of the world. He could not remember seeing anything beyond it, but did not know which was the truth, that his memory refused to tell him what was there, or that the castle had in reality stood in vacancy, on the brink of a void now quite filled with apple trees laid out in triangular patterns or as vast five-pointed stars. They were above the orchards still as they came down a slope to the castle, so that the patterns were clear, reaching as far as their eyes could see.

They went on downhill. The castle loomed up and soon filled all their vision. Around it was a bank of smooth green turf, and beyond that, a moat full of glassily green water, reflecting turrets and gates and towers and the grey stone of the walls. Jean saw Penn on his chestnut horse whose colour almost matched his own brilliant hair, ride ahead of them across the drawbridge. The archway beyond gathered him into its shadows, then hid him entirely. Otherwise there was nothing, no

sign, no sound, not a flicker of life from any opening or battlement, nor from anywhere. Insects had
ceased to sound, the lark – or any bird – to sing.
The seeming lack of life, however, was no more
oppressive than the heat of the sun. It was peaceful
and comfortable. And again, the silence was not a
negative but a positive force, not muffling sound,
but having a clarity which at once both heightened
sense and soothed it, healing Hugh's anxieties,
calming him as a salve might soothe a wound. The
very stones of the castle as they soaked up light,
transmitted calm, and now that Hugh was so much
closer he could see that they were less severely,
uncompromisingly grey; he could see green tones
and bluish-purple ones, and even in places a soft
pink one, like the tones in bare flesh.

They stepped on to the smooth green turf. It was
not in fact grass, but some close-cropped, thick and
curly plant which gave beneath their feet like moss,
and loosed simultaneously a powerful scent.

"It's camomile," said Jean, excitedly. "It's camomile, Hugh, did you realize? I've seen it at Kew.
It's what they've got on Buckingham Palace
lawns." Hugh's mind made a little, sharp, almost
external and totally ridiculous image of a scarlet-
coated guard in a sentry box up against the castle
wall. And then suddenly, as if someone had flicked
a switch, he had the same sense as he had the last
time he remembered coming into this world; of
being in two places at once; of doing two separate
things at once.

He was gliding up a long tunnel, underground.
He had no evidence for it being underground, but
knew for certain that it was. There was no sound,

not a footfall anywhere. Doors fell open smoothly
to let him pass. The ceilings and walls and floors
were of the same substance, glassy, reflecting,
though reflecting shapes rather than shadows and
images, but the doors that opened to him were at
once, and alternately, opaque and transparent;
when his eyes had accepted their transparency, they
would become suddenly opaque, when his eyes
had adjusted to their opaqueness they became again
transparent.

At the same time as this he was stepping on to
the drawbridge and walking across it. He could
feel it shake under his feet, and he had a sense of
echo, of hollowness beneath, but heard the sound
within his mind, not actually aloud. In a moment
they had left the drawbridge, had entered the
shadow beneath the archway, then passed out into
the light beyond. Looking back through the arch,
Hugh saw the world outside as a little bright snap-
shot, as infinitely remote as a holiday postcard.

He continued to walk in his glass tunnel. At the
same time this was now his other world, grey
walls, paving stones, beneath a sun that shone from
a soft blue sky; a benevolent eye, observing them.

The studs in the huge oak door were like eyes
too, as they had been before. Yet they were more
brilliant today than threatening, multiple brillianc-
ies, each stud reflecting another little bright sun
like the pupil in an eye, and together he saw now,
forming the same five-pointed star shapes as the
apple trees had. The bird handle of the door stared
out from among them as fiercely as ever. But its
eyes went beyond Hugh and Jean as if the enemy
lay elsewhere. The whole effect was of enormous

energy and splendour, the more so in their setting, that quiet grey court. Hugh turned the bird head, wrenching it with both his hands; and this time it moved and the door fell open. He felt himself sucked inside by some invisible, inaudible force and pulled Jean with him, after him. The door closed itself behind them.

He could not have said, then or afterwards from where his impression of energy, of furious movement came; because everything he saw, that printed itself so indelibly on his mind's eye that he was able to see it there for ever after, appeared as calm as what lay outside.

Till now his walk through the tunnel had coexisted with his journey into the castle. Now his two selves met and fused. He came into this inner courtyard from the outer one, he also came from his tunnel into the same place, though he had the impression of being pushed into it from behind, out of the tunnel, while he had seemed to be pulled, sucked in, from the outer court.

He stood there dazed and momentarily blinded.

The floor and walls of the court were like those of the tunnel, alternately transparent and opaque – at times Hugh could see through them to the apple trees beyond (which looked, though insubstantial, vague as a vision or a dream) at times they reflected back everything within the hall. At still other times, however, though they appeared transparent, he could see nothing beyond them but a faint blue haze. The castle might have been drifting in the sky; above, below and all round it, a huge void.

There was an apple tree in the middle of the court; strangely austere and stern, its leaves and trunk and branches seemed made of a dim silverish metal like pewter, and its apples of fine gold. A soft light came from these. It was more like electric than candle power in that it seemed less particular to its source than a candle flame would be, spreading itself further and more evenly, like light from electric bulbs. Yet it was also more mobile than electricity; ebbing and flowing within the fruit and within the hall, as living flames would move.

Beneath the apple tree stood a round bowl on a pedestal, like a baptismal font, but bigger. Anna stood beside it on a raised platform, and on the step below her knelt Penn, his hair like the golden apples, giving off light or appearing to. They were Penn and Anna and yet not Penn and Anna. "They're both grown up," said Jean in an awed voice, and indeed they were. Yet they looked exactly as they had known them, only the age and authority were new. Anna, though still small and pale beside her brother, had gained something of her mother's brilliance. It was a quieter, dimmer brilliance than her mother's, yet also fuller and more powerful; steel to silver, you could say. She wore the same clothes she had worn in their world, white shirt, black skirt, a medallion on a chain that Penn had bought her for her birthday from the cheap Indian shop in the town. But they might have been robes on her now, as Penn's clothes on him might have been armour.

Hugh's two kinds of knowledge fusing, he recognized them at last. Anna was not only Anna, but the girl in the alder grove (he even remembered that the Anna he knew had a nightdress as red as the dress in the alder grove). Penn was the man in armour who had passed him, riding, when he had been rooted, held to the willow tree.

Nothing except the apple tree was static. The fire threw light upon walls and floor, created lights and shadows which themselves constantly changed and shifted, taking on the forms of tree and flowers and of animals and birds, these reflected sometimes out into the sky itself. The sun had gone. The whole sky now was a dark, deep blue.

Hugh had to hold very tight to himself. He felt that if he did not he too would be lost, shifting shape from second to second. In a way he wanted to be lost. He wanted to let go, he would have done, yet something would not let him. Mostly that something could only have been Jean. She clung to his hand still, so holding him to his own form, he thought resentfully; she could not, would not, let him go.

Anna and Penn changed form, however. It might have been merely an illusion created by the shifting brilliance of the fire itself, yet at times they appeared indistinguishable from the form it took. At one moment Anna became a giantess, her head lost in darkness, shadows falling from her out-stretched arms across the bodies of Jean and Hugh. The next moment she dwindled to her own size. Penn dwindled too. Briefly he was the Penn they knew; but he did not remain there, he went on dwindling, until a tiny baby lay at Anna's feet; their baby, as if new-born again.

He heard Jean gasp beside him, as Anna bent and took the baby up. For a moment she held him close to her. Then she stretched out her arms, the baby hung above the flames. Hugh knew what would happen then. But he did not let it disturb him, not least because he wanted it to happen; that was his decision, he wanted it; he wanted it to happen to him, too, because thereafter he would have to decide nothing; it would all be done. All he must do now was wait and see what came of it.

But Jean's grip on his hand tightened. "Hugh. *Hugh.* You must stop her. She's going to put him in the fire."

Anna had never appeared smaller or more ordinary. She was even chewing her tongue, Hugh saw. But it did not make her any less powerful.

"Don't you see. She has to put him on the fire," he said, his voice thick in his throat. "That's the point of the cupboard. Don't you see."

"No, I don't see," Jean screamed. "She'll burn him. She'll burn him to death."

"Not to death," said Hugh. "To life. Isn't that right, Anna?" He appealed to her directly now. She took the baby to her breast again and in her most little girl voice said to Jean, not to him.

"I'm going to burn him, Jean. I'm going to make him live for ever. We can all live for ever if we want."

"I don't want to live for ever," Jean screamed. "Nor does Penn. Nor does Hugh."

Anna turned to Hugh now. Anna, not Anna, she said, she almost wheedled in the way he most disliked in the Anna he knew – he had heard her talk to Penn like that, when she wanted her own way – "You don't want to die do you, Hugh? You don't want to get old do you? *I* don't want to get old. I don't want my skin to shrivel and my hair to turn white. I don't want Penn's to, or yours. I want you both to stay with me in my castle." Her voice coaxed him now; very slow, very low. "All I have to do is bathe him in the fire, then bathe you. Don't want to get old, Hugh. Don't want to die."

"Don't listen to her, Hugh," said Jean; sensible Jean; in a voice he knew in her, too, and didn't like much better. "Don't listen to her. Listen to me."

"Don't listen to her, Hugh. Listen to me," said Anna. She still held the baby over the flame. But now he saw, to his horror, she would do nothing till he said; it was he who had to make up his mind; Anna had made up her mind; Jean had made up hers. And now it was his, Hugh's turn. He had bought the cupboard after all; it was his. He had to decide the whole thing for himself.

But now it came to it, he did not know what he wanted. It would have been easy without Jean there, he would have just nodded his head, Anna could do as she was urging, what was it to him? Yet it was not a question of whether he wanted to die one day or not. It was a question of making up his mind about it. And he did not know where or what his mind was. Even had it been working properly, his body would not work, it was rooted, paralysed again, just as the willow tree had paralysed it. Just as his mind was paralysed. He could not connect any one thought to another, nor hold to a single logical thread. There were only two choices after all and each repeated itself over and over, yet each repetition was different from before as well as the same. Stop Anna; let her. Save Penn;

leave him. Walk in to the fire, don't walk into the fire – these were the thoughts went chasing through his head, one after another, time after time. Allow; do nothing. Do nothing; allow. Yet each time it sounded fresh and new. The choice astonished him. His own consciousness was the single link. His mind had to make the decision, to snap the succession at one idea, so inhibiting the next, but even if his mind had been able to do so, his body would not have obeyed. With a huge effort of will, he managed at last to think, fleetingly, of Penn, his friend, of his friendship for Anna too, surprisingly, with this other Anna wheedling him from the other side of the fire. He thought of Jean. For a moment he thought of himself. Avalon, he thought. Thomas the Rhymer, he thought. He remembered all those people taken to live with the fairies, or with the Gods or with Arthur, for ever and ever. And then, pushing these thoughts aside, he thought of the old man's many lives, and of his own house and his bedroom and the ash tree in the garden. He thought of Humbert, the cat.

Thereafter all thought blurred, one thought lost itself in the next. Hugh felt he was a tree now. He felt rooted, fibrous, with branches; with sap flowing through him, through every vein. He could feel the whole of him, tree self, human self, his human body like one drawn by an old-fashioned anatomist; he felt the paths and strength of each vein and bone and muscle. He held up his hand and against the bone of the fire it looked transparent. He could see the glow of blood and the bones of his fingers, knobbed at the knuckles. He reached his hand out to Anna for help. She reached the baby towards him, nearer and nearer the fire. The flames touched both of them; nearly touched both of them. Avalon. Avalon. The ash tree. Humbert, the kitten-cat.

"Hugh. Hugh. Oh *Hugh*." Jean was screaming at him now, was pulling him, punching him, shaking him, to no effect. There ran in his head still, unstoppable – Stop Anna. Let her. Avalon. Humbert the cat. I am a tree. I am . . . But Jean was still screaming away besides him, she was fumbling at her brooch, the brown stone in its silver setting. She undid it at last, pulled it out, she jabbed its pin into his arm with all her strength. "*Hugh*!" she screamed one more time. And at the sudden, agonizing pain, Hugh screamed too; his mind cleared momentarily by the pain and fright, he gathered all his strength, snapped the succession, snatched one thought out and held it there as if in front of him, fed his voice with it. "Stop, Anna, no," he said, slowly, thickly. It was hardly a decision, more a pressure to which he had at last acceded; whether it was what he truly wanted he did not know. It didn't even seem to matter very much. His voice might have belonged to someone else. "Stop, Anna," it said. "No, Anna. Don't."

The words stilled everything. They stilled the fire, the leaping shadows, they stilled Anna's arms, they stilled the world turning about the transparent walls of the court. They stilled his thoughts. The only movement left belonged to Jean – once made, predictable, unexceptional as it was, it suppressed all other movements, all other possibilities. Anna, standing by the dying fire, looked small and pale and harmless, a little girl; all the energy having left her, as it had left this place, she let Jean take the baby from her, without let, without hindrance. Hugh's mind, too, was a vacuum. He felt insubstantial, a thin pale shell, that would shatter at a touch.

Jean went ahead of him now, towards the inner door of the castle. Holding the baby close to her, Anna at her heels, she walked as if she was asleep. Hugh went after them, slowly. His eyes on Anna's feet, he saw that the strap on her right sandal had come away from the sole, so that her foot kept losing it, sliding sideways, out of the shoe.

They had almost reached the door. Behind them as Hugh turned to look for the last time, he saw that the fire in the bowl had died. The silvered apple tree was on fire instead, a tree of flame, but a cold, consuming flame, as icy as the stars.

They walked through the great door of the castle into a void. It felt like walking off the edges of the world. Hugh expected to find himself falling, and for a moment sensed infinite distance and infinite time, sound growing from him, flowing round him, spreading infinitely, echoing.

The void narrowed and the echo died. The sound compressed itself, folded itself in, clattered as if against a closed and wooden wall. There was a sudden, blinding light. The cupboard door opened, all four of them walked out onto Hugh's bedroom floor; Hugh, Jean, Anna and lastly Penn in his proper age and form.

The void had gone. Walls had closed round Hugh, confining him, imprisoning him in the narrowest of castles; the castle of bone, he thought. This castle of bone was himself.

CHAPTER SIXTEEN

It was the same but different. They were the same four people but different.

It was Penn who was the hardest to accept. They had known him both as a new-born baby and as a man, and at his present size, much nearer man than baby he still looked surprisingly small. It was like coming into a house you had known as a young child, huge in memory now appearing to have shrunk, both in size and in effect. It made Hugh feel diminished – almost cheated too. On the other hand if he thought of the baby, Penn seemed gigantic; his arms and legs quite grossly thick, like trees.

He stood in the middle of Hugh's room now, head down, shaking it, totally bewildered, believing nothing. That was his protection and relief. If he remembered the castle or what had happened he deliberately refused to admit he had. He protested indignantly when they showed him the empty jars of baby food, the bottle with the inch of milk left in the bottom; indeed, looking at Penn now Hugh found them quite as astonishing himself. And when they tried to tell him that it was no longer Thursday, that a whole day had passed, he would not accept this at first, merely grew angrier. They had to turn on Radio One (rather a coming and going sound because Hugh's transistor needed batteries) to prove it to him. An excited voice said "Hullo everyone, *hullo*. It's one o'clock again and welcome to our Friday Show. We've got some great, *great* sounds for you today" – that it was still only one o'clock giving Hugh almost as great a shock as the fact that it was undeniably Friday must have given Penn. While they were in the cupboard no time had passed outside.

They turned off the radio and heard another, though differently excited voice coming from their hall. "Hugh, Jean. *Lunch*. You said five minutes." "Coming," Hugh yelled back, to placate it temporarily.

Penn had to believe this now, that it was Friday; but immediately shut the knowledge out, or rather the fact that it meant anything peculiar. When Anna said "You were a *lovely* baby, Penn," mocking him, and Jean followed in all seriousness "Oh yes, you were smashing *really*, Penn," he lowered his head again and shook it again violently, as if he was trying to shake something from his eyes.

"Shut up. Shut *up*." His voice tailed off – Hugh had never seen him less in command of things. That made him feel less safe, less protected too, and again he felt cheated.

He got Anna, alone, into a corner.

"What happened? Did you understand?" he asked. "Why, didn't you?" "I suppose I did," he said. "Glad we got Penn back then?" "Yes . . . aren't you?" "Of course. Or I guess so." There was not doubt exactly in what they said, but a kind of dissociation certainly.

"It would have been different without Jean," Anna said.

"Yes," said Hugh. Then he added, remembering suddenly, "The old man said she was important. Maybe that was what he meant."

"Maybe the old man didn't want us to stay," said Anna.

"Maybe he was warning us against it," said Hugh. "Maybe he didn't like living for so long."

"Maybe he'll die now," said Anna, "Without the cupboard."

"Maybe he's dead already," Hugh said. But Anna, he saw, wasn't listening any more.

"Oh blast, I've broken my sandal," she said, taking it off to examine it. "Do you think it's mendable?" The strap had parted from the sole itself, Hugh thought it would be difficult. "Well if it isn't going to be any more use *anyway*," Anna said, and she marched to the cupboard, put the sandal on the shelf and shut the door. The attention of the others centred on to her. They stood and watched in silence, even Penn. Hugh felt properly that he ought to be alarmed but was not alarmed at all, and when Anna pulled open the cupboard door and the sandal lay there unchanged, he knew why, that he had not expected it to change. Penn was smiling now with Jean. He looked more confident already.

"I'm going for a pee," he said, and disappeared downstairs. Jean began putting Hugh's clothes on the cupboard shelves.

"Well that's it then," she said, at last closing the cupboard door. "You won't have any excuse now, Hugh, not to keep your clothes tidy." At which he felt a surge of mindless, maniacal anger. "Can't you think of anything except tidying?" he bawled at her. It was a relief to feel so angry, yet afterwards again, almost immediately, he felt nothing.

"Hugh, Jean, *lunch*!" Their mother's voice

sounded frantic. They went downstairs and Penn
took Anna home.

But that was not quite all. In practical terms there
was still plenty to be done. Hugh did it with bore-
dom, but glad in a way that his mind was not
required. The litter from the baby and from the
other transformations of the cupboard had created
an extraordinary jumble, which he sorted alone,
rejumbled and threw into the dustbin. Jean seemed
reluctant to help him. He saw less and less of Penn
and Anna.

For almost the whole of that holidays things kept
on turning up, pieces of stone or metal, dried up
pine-needles, wood shavings, other traces of what
had passed. He even found eventually, in the
pocket of his jeans, the apple he had picked for
Jean. It was mummified, quite dry, as if centuries
old, and stirred in him a curious and not at all
pleasant unease. Everything he found stirred him
in some way, gave him pain, a sense of loss; yet it
was a fading progression, each time the pain was
a little less. He did not like this, tried to reanimate
the feeling, but to no avail, logic opposing memory
with increasing efficiency. He could not feel the
loss of magic because, almost, he did not believe
in it any more. Yet in an odd way he was still
afraid of it, of magic.

He did not go back to the shop. He avoided even
going past it, though his father told him once that
it had closed. "I suppose the old boy must have
died," he said.

The living evidence remained, of course. The
kitten, Humbert, had to go once more through all

the processes of growing-up, including neutering. He mewed piteously the night he came home from the vet's, as well he might, poor beast, thought Hugh sympathetically, just think of having to have that done to you twice, but nothing now would impede his progression to old age; after a while everyone seemed to forget that he had repeated his beginning.

As for the tortoise Hugh found a box for it to live in and fed it on lettuce and let it out sometimes on the lawn. He became quite fond of it, and so did Jean. But after three or four weeks it vanished from the garden, mysteriously and they never saw it again. "I haven't even got my box," mourned Jean.

Hugh gave his mother the lemon soap, and on that same day, towards the end of the holidays, he was wrapping rubbish in an old copy of the local newspaper when his eye fell on a heading.

PARK PIG MYSTERY

Mr Frederick Jameson (40) Chief Ranger employed by the Parks Commission was surprised last Sunday to find a large white pig roaming in the park near Fenn lakes. The pig, a sow, and by her appearance recently a mother, had not been reared in the park. To add to the mystery, the mark stamped on the animal's back proved to be that of a farm in North Shropshire no longer in existence.

Neither Mr Jameson nor other park officials could explain the pig's sudden appearance. Nor has any other explanation been forthcoming. The only clues to the mystery lie in reports of a pig having been seen earlier in Regina Road, passers-by wrongly assuming that the animal had escaped from the park.

"Pigs have not been reared in the park within living memory," stated Mr Jameson. "We can only assume that someone locally has been keeping a pig in unapproved premises, and has not come forward to claim the animal for fear of prosecution. The Police have been informed."

The *Shuttered Room*

by Christine Purkis

Open up THE SHUTTERED ROOM, a compelling story of love - and hate - by Christine Purkis.

Life is sweet for Alison. A long, hot summer nannying in France is bound to brush up her French, top up her tan and - who knows? - maybe even pep up her love life too! But things aren't so simple, as Alison quickly discovers...

'My God! This is terrible!'

The words sounded loud, strange in this silent room.

At first she felt she wanted to do something. She sprang up and went to the window. Rain drops were sprinkling down, though the real storm was still rumbling over the other side of the valley.

It was here, she found herself thinking. It was here. I know it. It has to be. On this bed. These curtains... a night like this... I can't sleep in here! she thought wildly.

But as she stood in the room, staring at the crumpled quilt, at the impression of her own body where she had just been lying, she knew she had no choice.

RED FOX paperback, £3.50 ISBN 0 09 947231 7

THE
SNOW-WALKER
SEQUENCE

Book 1

CATHERINE FISHER

THE **SNOW-WALKER'S SON**

Short-listed for the WH Smith Mind Boggling Books Award

*S*ome say he's a monster, others hope he is
dead, and no one has seen him for many,
many years. Until now...

'I'm sending you to live with my son,' the Jarl said.

For a moment they couldn't realize what he meant.
Then Jessa felt sick; cold sweat prickled on her back.

Thorkil was white. 'You can't send us there,' he
breathed.

'Hold your tongue and let me finish.' Ragnar was
looking at them now, with a hard, amused stare.

'Call it exile, and think yourselves lucky. At least you'll
have a sort of life. You leave tomorrow for Thrasirshall, at
first light.'

Jessa saw Thorkil was trembling. She knew he couldn't
believe this; he was terrified. It burst out of him in a wild
despairing cry.

'I won't go! You can't send us out there, not to that
creature!'

Out now in paperback from Red Fox at £3.50
1 THE SNOW-WALKER'S SON, ISBN 0 09 925192 2
2 THE EMPTY HAND, ISBN 0 09 925182 5
3 THE SOUL THIEVES, ISBN 0 09 953971 3

THE *Herring Girls*

*T*heresa Tomlinson blends fact with fiction in her moving account of thirteen-year-old Dory, caught up in the close-knit, hard-working fishing community of Whitby. Dory's determined to be a strong, fast worker – but has she got what it takes to be a real herring girl?

Here's a preview to get you hooked...

I took the sharpest knife from my pocket and picked up a good-sized fish, trying hard to remember what Hannah had taught me. I pushed the knife in carefully and twisted it, and the guts flew out into the gut tub.

The man grunted. 'Now size?' he snapped.

'Mattiefull,' I answered him, my voice all shaky.

'What?' He put his hand to his ear.

'Mattiefull,' I said loudly.

He nodded and pointed to the basket behind me. I slipped the fish in and snatched up another herring to gut.

Nelly pushed in beside me and set to work. Mary Jane went to pack the barrel behind us.

I paused to watch Nelly for a moment and my mouth dropped open. Nelly could certainly gip, and she could gip fast. She'd done four fish while I did one.

'Stop gawping,' she muttered under her breath. 'Get gipping!'

RED FOX paperback, £3.50, ISBN 0 09 936311 9